Anastasius Grün

The Last Knight

A romance-garland

Anastasius Grün

The Last Knight
A romance-garland

ISBN/EAN: 9783337064730

Printed in Europe, USA, Canada, Australia, Japan

Cover: Foto ©Andreas Hilbeck / pixelio.de

More available books at **www.hansebooks.com**

A ROMANCE-GARLAND.

FROM THE GERMAN OF ANASTASIUS GRÜN.

TRANSLATED, WITH NOTES, BY

JOHN O. SARGENT.

NEW YORK:

PUBLISHED BY HURD AND HOUGHTON.

Cambridge: Riverside Press.

1871.

TO

OLIVER WENDELL HOLMES

IN MEMORY OF YOUNG DAYS NOW

OLD TIMES,

THIS VOLUME IS INSCRIBED BY

HIS FRIEND

JOHN O. SARGENT

INTRODUCTION.

ANASTASIUS GRÜN is the poetical pseudonym of Count ANTON ALEXANDER VON AUERSPERG, who was born April 11, 1806, at Laibach in the Austrian duchy of Craniola. His father died early and left him the family estates at Gurkfeld, and the Castle of Thurn-am-Hart. He was educated in philosophy and jurisprudence at Vienna, where he went in his childhood and remained till his twenty-fourth year, passing only his vacations at the rural homestead. He afterwards lived alternately at Vienna and on his estates, making occasional journeys into France, North and South Germany, Italy, and Belgium. In 1838 he married the Countess Maria Attems, daughter of the Governor-general of Styria. Ten years later he was sent by the estates and the men of letters of Austria to the German *Vor-Parlament*, and was then elected by the circle of Laibach to the National Assembly, which he left in the autumn of the same year, without having taken a very active part in their proceedings. On some important questions he voted with the Left Centre. At Frankfort he was the witness of stormy scenes, and after the catastrophe of the eighteenth September (when his fellow-members, Major Auerswald and Prince Lichnowski, were murdered by the mob), he seems to have retired from public life. Regarded as the head of the liberal party, his opinions exposed him to the attentions of the Austrian police, and he was fined five and twenty ducats (afterwards remitted) for the violation of the ordinance that forbade the publication of anything by an Austrian, even in a foreign country, without previously submitting it to the domestic censorship. He was unjustly accused of having changed his political professions, in order to obtain a seat in the House of Lords, which enabled him with his wife to appear at court.

After publishing several minor pieces in the almanacs — at that time a usual channel for the production of rising authors, — he appeared for the first time, in 1830, in a volume of collected poems entitled "Blätter der Liebe." These poems were said by the critics to be written in the prevailing Austrian vein, with a strong dash of HEINE. The same year he published at Stuttgart "Der Letzte Ritter," THE LAST KNIGHT, — a series of ballads founded on incidents in the life of the Emperor MAXIMILIAN I., — and forming a national poem, which gave him immediate and wide reputation. His fame was increased by the "Spaziergänge eines Wiener Poeten," political lyrics, that well deserved the celebrity they attained. These works, with his other productions — "Schutt," "Gedichte," "Nibelungen im Frack," and "Pfaff Vom Kahlenberg," — exhibiting powers of humor and irony no less than a high order of imagination, and great vigor and beauty of expression, entitled him to rank, and have maintained his position among the best and most distinguished of the living poets of Germany.

CONTENTS.

THE LAST KNIGHT.

CONTENTS.

The Last Knight.

The Ruler's Cradle.

(1459.)

WHITHER, thou sad companion? And cripples, whither ye?
Whither, ye riders? Whither, thou sailor of the sea?
Whether sailing, limping, riding, all are bound to Kingdom Come,
While I am making coffins for you and me at home."

Hard by the Castle of Neustadt, in a joiner's house, this song
In hollow clang resounding, may be heard the whole day long;
The youthful master sings it, as soon as the morning glows,
With the fresh lips of boyhood, where the first down scarcely blows.

There enter'd once this workshop, in joyful haste, a man—
"A cradle make, my master, as quickly as you can;
Good luck to Emperor Frederick, and the crown by his father worn,
Leonor', the haughty Empress,[1] this day a son has borne."

The joiner makes the cradle from scantling strong and dry,
From the same scantling fashion'd a coffin stands hard by;
Around fly the chips and splinters, saw creaks, and hammer rings,
Meanwhile his old-time ditty the youthful master sings.

In the castle chapel a baptistry of polished marble gleams,
Whence to-day on the brow of an infant the holy water streams;
Now rises the Bishop of Salzburg, and heavenward lifts his eyes,
"This infant—Maximilian—in God's name, I baptize."

Oh, Leonor'! Oh, Frederick! until this happy day,
The stars on your alliance have shed no placid ray:
Lisboa's stately daughter now looks fondly in his face,
And clasps the royal craven with a womanly embrace.

Around the cradle the courtiers in a gorgeous circle lean,
That the boy may be used thus early to the splendour of such a scene;
While over the child bends Leonor', to fondle it and to kiss,
Forgetting she is a princess, in the flush of a mother's bliss.

I see two strangers standing the throng of courtiers nigh,
Guests to my vision palpable, but to no other eye;
One of them is a woman, who in beauty's bloom appears,
The other an ancient wizard, wither'd and bent by years.

Death, in the tongue of mortals, the meagre old man is hight,
And Life is the name of the woman, so beautiful and bright;
With silent steps, and viewless, the twain through the circle glide,
And to Life, pale Death, the grey-beard, thus speaks by the cradle's
side.

"The threads of this child's destiny, say, which of us shall twine?
The boy will be a monarch, and therefore be he mine!
The boy will be a monarch, and alike, whether bad or good,
Never died on earth a monarch free from the stain of blood.

"Of the world and its sweet allurements he nothing knows as yet,
It will be to him no anguish if my seal on his brow is set;
Well for him should he depart now, for his heart would never know,
Haply, the pangs of royalty, or the pangs of human woe.

"Were his eyes closed now, were his pulses never to throb again,
It might spare the immolation of whole hecatombs of men;
A thousand eyes might be smiling he would make with weeping red,
And a thousand gardens blooming he would people with the dead.

"If now this brain were wither'd, it were spared the contemplation
Of the graves that may be needed to lay a throne's foundation;
If this blood stop now, the blood of his people will not stream
To colour the purple which haply to his eye too pale may seem.

"It is the fate of humanity, that monarchs should cause men grief;
And were he vouchsafed by heaven of the world's best kings the chief,
He must sometime cause his people to know the bitterest smart,
When Fate in the midst of his greatness stops the pulses of his heart."

And Death is mute. In the circle his utterance no one heard,
But as he spoke, the heart's blood grew cold with every word,
The flowers at the window wilting, around their pale leaves lie;
And his first unconscious tear-drops bedew the infant's eye.

"Now in the veins of this infant shall the heart's blood cease to flow?
Shall his eyes be shorn of their lustre, and his cheeks grow pale?
Ah, No!
As the son of Life I claim him—mine shall the boy be, mine!
My kiss is on his forehead—my arms his limbs entwine!

"He shall become a monarch in the world's imperial strife;
Crown'd and enthroned, the monarch is the chosen son of Life;
The cities now in ashes from their ruins he uprears,
From the eyes that now are weeping he wipes away the tears.

"He gladly plucks the laurel, and the wreath of evergreen,
To circle the brow of manhood with its unfading sheen;
He lifts the lofty steeple, and spreads the ample nave,
Where sepulchres are yawning, and grave-yard grasses wave.

"The people's weal is the pillow whereon he sleeps softly by night,
The people's hearts are the columns that sustain his throne aright;
The columns seem ever too few for him, the pillow seems ever too
small,
His faith is the strength of his sceptre, his charity reacheth all.

"And as the sunbeams visibly, invisibly there breathe
Soft airs from the throne of the monarch, that bless the lands
beneath;
Concord dwells in the palace, and content the cottage fills;
Peace trills in the songs of the valleys, and freedom blows from the
hills.

" As the larks in tuneful chorus warble out in the morning sky,
So for him breathing their orisons a thousand souls heavenward
fly ;
And blessings shall still float upward from the spot where his ashes
lie ;
This is the work of a monarch, and this be his destiny !"

Life speaks in a voice of triumph, on her brow a glory appears,
Though as none in the circle sees her, so none in the circle hears ;
But the larks break forth in a carol, through the fields spring airs
blow mild,
And the first gentle smile of gladness flits over the lips of the child.

And as the child, so around him the attending courtiers smile,
But the Emperor, lost in reflection, the circle leaves the while :
Going forth with the astrologers, the old men and the wise,
To read the infant's future in the letters of the skies.

More warmly Leonora, and yet more warmly press'd,
To her heart the tender infant, and cradled him on her breast ;
In his twin eyes fondly gazing with a mother's look divine,
" Ye stars of my good fortune, thus ever on me shine !"

The Young Prince.

(TRANSITION.)

A VINE-DRESSER has planted at his cottage door a vine,
And fresh in the sun of spring-time its tender leaflets shine;
Full soon the little plant joyfully tosses its rich green leaves,
And gives spring and earth its greeting, and the greeting it gives—receives.

And spring-time follows on spring-time, and boldly its tendrils aspire,
And the stem throws out its branches, which ever climb higher and higher;
And with richer growth and richer its foliage sways in the air,
And its green arms fondly shelter the earliest clusters there.

On a shaft the vine-dresser trains it, whereto it may safely cling;
But in the air, proudly and freely, it loves by itself to swing:
And spring-time follows on spring-time, and the foliage, lush and green,
Creeps over the vine-dresser's cottage, and covers it like a screen;

And arches itself to a cupola, where the matted foliage strays,
And arches itself to an arbour where cluster on cluster sways;
Around fly the birds and warble the little songs sweet to hear,
For where the grapes are abounding, the singers are sure to be near!

And what a joy and a blessing to the vine-dresser and his wife,
When they see the scion expanding, so full of beauty and life;
While in the embower'd cottage dwell friendship, love and content,
And the clink of glasses with psalmody and voices of mirth is blent.

Oh, Leonor' and Frederick! the years in pleasure glide,
As your son matures in beauty and in stature by your side;
As he from child to stripling, to youth from boyhood grows,
In his heart the warmth of spring-time and on his cheek the rose!

How of the world regardless you see the unthinking boy,
When his father's crown is nothing to him but a shining toy:
How life's problem is unfolded as the years his cheeks embrown,
And he reads the mystic meaning of the Cross upon the Crown.

How the pedant, who would drill him in the jargon of the schools,
Finds a mind he cannot shackle with the rigour of his rules;
While he, who light and wisdom and justice would impart,
Finds a seed-time and a harvest in the garden of his heart.

Frederick looks on him with wonder and shakes his naked head,
As a lame man sees the dancers the mazy circle tread,
But the heart of Leonora is with pride and rapture wild,
As she whispers oft—there's nothing of the father in the child!

How lordly, son of princes, in crowded life you rise,
The beams of hope he drinketh who looks into your eyes;
You find your brilliant image in the gorgeous morning cloud,
Lit with the golden glory its veiling mists enshroud.

You are a spring full of flowers that in the bud cradled lie,
A heaven of constellations, shut out by a clouded sky:
You are a sea full of pearls hid under the billowy brine,
A mountain full of diamonds, still buried in the mine.

Hail, when your day once calleth! the Orient in a blaze,
Flowers, stars, and pearls, and diamonds flash out in the sun's first
rays;
Then shower not on your people as alms your morning light,
Which their long and hopeful waiting makes a duty and a right.

Austria and Burgundy.

(1475.)

I. CHARLES THE BOLD.

T Trèves there sit[2] two Princes over their golden wine,
No courtiers lounge there listening, and only the lustre's shine
Betrays a wrinkled forehead where a royal crown reposes,
And a youthful visage radiant with smiles enwreathed in roses.

One, a melancholy hero, is rich in deeds of fame,
And one, like a young cedar, fresh and vigorous of frame;
The one seems a day of Autumn, which brings home the yellow fruit,
The other a Spring morning, that quickens the germ and root.

One is like the mossy oak-tree, at whose trunk the woodman stands;
The other, a tender sapling, needs the gardener's training hands;
One seems the sun at its setting in the crimson surge of the West,
The other the star of Love beaming with smiles on the Orient's crest.

It seems to the earnest hero that afresh his spring-time blows,
When the eye of his young companion with native ardour glows;
And the air round the youth seems rustling with the sweep of
Time's swift pinion,
As his serious friend discourses of kingcraft and dominion.

The one is rich in victories, and rest is now his aim,
The other plans achievements to win him future fame;
The one is call'd the Bold in all Burgundy, the other
All Germans know as "Austria's Max," and love him like a
brother.

Each at the other gazes, and presses hand in hand,
While, fill'd to the brim beside them, the golden goblets stand;
And Friendship's rosy fingers the faithful colours blend,
To paint on the heart of either the likeness of his friend.

Like an image of the Virgin upon an oak-tree laid,
So gleams on Charles's bosom the image of a maid,

Like himself, as the reflection of the sun is in the sea,
Which softer than its counterpart and milder well may be.

The sun the eye may dazzle, not its image in the water,
So Max looks long and gladly on the portrait of the daughter;
And when with Charles's goblet his own together clinks,
He can hardly say for certain whose health it is he drinks.'

In the morning, as the Princes are about to bid adieu,
Warm heart to warm heart pressing, it was beautiful to view
Their warriors gathering round them, and clasping hand in hand,
While the rosy dawn with its blushes suffuses all the land.

II. CHARLES'S DEATH.

THE moon looks down on lovely lands, in traversing the skies,
But joyously o'er Burgundy she stops to feast her eyes;
The sun who dallies gallantly with ladies north and south,
Is never tired of kissing Burgundian Mary's mouth.

Rich is the Duke of Burgundy in beautiful domains;
Purple clusters gem the hill-tops, and yellow sheaves the plains;
Rich cities and free peoples in the streams reflected shine,
And Bliss is here the reaper, and Plenty trims the vine.

Earth strives with all her treasures his possessions to environ,
His lands abound in quarries, and in mines of lustrous iron;
For him full many a castle in pride and splendour looms,
And in the golden castle a lovely daughter blooms.

With a sword in battle temper'd he must defend his lands,
That their gardens may not wither in the smoke of hostile brands;
He must protect these treasures, to flourish and increase
Long after their true guardian in the grave-yard rests in peace.

"Farewell! if I return not, my daughter, calm thy fears,
And bathe in a new sun-light the spring-time of thy years;
In Austria may it shine on thee, and wealth of blessings shower,
In a pride that brooks no rival there blooms the hero-flower."

Gazing after him intently the weeping daughter stands,
As the gallant father sallies forth with his intrepid bands;
Like the thunder and the lightning in the clefts of clouded skies,
See the flash of glittering weapons, and hark the battle cries!

By Nancy, for the ravens is a carnival in store,
Sits the Duke in bloody judgment, who never will judge more!
There the hero-tree of Burgundy was prostrate, branch and stem,
Flowers of Lorraine and Switzerland—the same blast wither'd them!

Mark the colours and the crests which the hosts opposing show,
Mark the crests and colours mingled where the slaughter'd hosts lie low:
Like kings in purple mantles with smoking carnage red—
Know you who has thus united them? Death reconciles the dead!

At Nancy a new tombstone in the Cathedral lies,
And o'er it like a statue leans a maid with weeping eyes;
On her countenance is brooding a sorrow dark and deep,
One here may see a daughter for a loving father weep.

At Nancy in the grave-yard a multitude appear,
Led by the ties of sorrow from districts far and near:
And if any tears are shed there, they without deception fall—
The mourners, as they bury us, adjudge the deeds of all!

III. THE MESSAGE.

MAX alone in meditation in his silent chamber reads,
He thinks of the words of sages, and cons heroic deeds;
When greeting comes a messenger, of a strange sort, forsooth;
What news may he be bringing to the imperial youth?

One could not well conjecture if his news were good or bad,
He wore the garb of mourning—but his countenance was glad;
As the angel of death approaches, like a messenger of wrath,
But smiling, kisses the sufferer, and points to a rosy path.

"From a maid I bring you greeting, the sweetest maid can send,
And the last kiss of remembrance from an old departed friend:
I was sent to you from Nancy, and I came upon the wing,
And with me this little letter, in charge to you I bring."

To Max thus spake the messenger. "Oh, mayst thou come from one"—
Max whispers, "whom I think of, and whom I love alone!
Though mine eye has not beheld her, in her alone I trust,
As in the unseen heaven, and the glory of the just."

He oped the letter silently—therein a gold ring lay,
Whence the sapphire and the diamond sent forth a blended ray;
And a grey lock lay beside it—red with blood was many a hair,—
Words sad to him, words dear to him, that little letter share.

"He was friend to us, and father—who beneath the gravestone
sleeps,
Where a daughter in affliction for him who loved us weeps,
In joy, in woe, he thought of thee—thus think of him, I pray,
And next thy heart preserve it, this precious lock of grey.

"Thine by the choice of my father, my heart's choice rests on thee,
Then take this little ring of gold, though poor and frail it be;
It will answer for a token, when thou comest I will know,
By the blue shine of the sapphire, and the diamond's liquid glow."

Max kiss'd the ring and the ringlet, his heart in sad eclipse,
"Oh, Charles, and oh, my Mary"—still dwell upon his lips;
"Oh, silver star of friendship, thy course ends bloody red!
Oh, star of love, how thou risest, so golden overhead!"

Then an o'erflowing tear-drop which from his eyelids roll'd,
Fell on the lock of grey and the little ring of gold;
Was it born of pain or pleasure, the tear that dimm'd his eyes?
Your heart indeed may guess it, but I may not surmise![2]

IV. THE RENDEZVOUS.

THE feather'd choir returning in gladsome chorus sing,
And the buds outpeeping timidly inaugurate the spring;
When Max and the Duke of Bavaria for a stroll in the green fields start,
And the Prince to his friend lays open the secret of his heart:

"My Louis, how superbly life buds and blooms around,
What notes of busy gladness from hut and palace sound!
With the germs of spring returning, love's messengers appear,
And you shall be the messenger of greeting to my dear.

"Hie hence to Mary of Burgundy, and my obeisance make,
And then as my loyal legate her hand at the altar take;
To the bridal couch attend her,—nay, rogue, you must not smile.
For your loyalty requires you to be clad in mail the while.

"Your right leg cased in steel, and in steel vour right arm cased,
With a keen edge and shining—a sword between you placed;
This means, woe to the traitor who our sacred bond would sever,
That means, in peace and war her name is my legend ever."

Rides off the Duke of Bavaria—he is jubilant and gay,
All are smiling, priest or soldier, who meet him on the way,
And citizen and peasant rejoicingly admires,
And the handsome Duchess of Burgundy in the country of her sires!

Before the gates of Ghent clouds of dust the entrance veil,
Where banners float, flash weapons, and glisten coats of mail;
There's a tramping and a stamping where the horses paw the ground,
There's a singing and a ringing where the warriors' shouts resound

Through the city's crowded avenues the cavalcade proceeds,
Nine hundred German nobles, in armour, on their steeds;
In their midst behold a stripling his chestnut charger rein;
Why thronging thus around him do the people all remain?

He is dress'd in simple armour, but a coronet of pearls,
Sole emblem of distinction, bedecks his yellow curls,
Is it this then, or the brightness which flashes in his eye,
That challenges the homage of every passer-by?

Forth issues then the Duchess to meet the cavalcade,
Her countenance the mirror in which beauty is arrayed;
In her raven ringlets gleaming a cluster of diamonds bright,
Like a living constellation set in the swarthy night.

She look'd the youthful hero in his shining eye of blue,
"Ha! the pure flash of the diamond, and the sapphire's azure
hue!"
Then upon his golden tresses a long regard she bent,
"You bring me a thousand ringlets for the little ring I sent."

She sinks on his manly bosom, and yields to a chaste embrace,
"Come to my heart, thou scion of a noble German race."
Max was the happy youth, you would hardly need be told,—
She knew from the sapphire and diamond, and the little ring of gold.

In air and wood already the voice of the singers was spent,
But the tones of the harp resounded still in the palace of Ghent;
And if moon and stars were thinking by themselves to take the air,
They found in the palace gardens two others their walk to share.

In the palace joy carouses as the mountain torrent raves,
Love whispers in the gardens, like the flow of summer waves ;
The Wood believes that whispering is his exclusive right ;
To such a tale one pair at least will give the lie to-night !

One only hears their whispers, who high in ether dwells,
And she who knows the secret is the only one who tells—
She told me (confidentially) the whole of what she heard,
Thus the moon, the stars' pale keeper, mine ancient friend, averr'd.

"Oh, were we but two planets which near each other glow,
Oh, were we but two clouds which soft airs together blow,
We should look then on the earth as the Now on Long Ago,
As Liberty on Fetters, as Happiness on Woe.

"We would be indeed two flowers which rejoice the heart and eye,
With their perfume and their beauty, of all who saunter by ;
We would gaze on one another and on the sun in the sky,
And when we fade to heaven on the wings of zephyrs fly.

"Then from the empyrean, on the earth which was our home,
We would smilingly contemplate our cradle and our tomb,"—
So they prattle and they rattle as lovers always do,
If you've loved you understand it, and if not, the worse for you.

The wind is quite too civil their chat to discompose—
As if it trod on tip-toe the streamlet gently flows;
Mute are the gossip poplars, though they love to say their say—
Hush, ye sisters, for to-morrow there will be another day.

Through the hall with friendly greetings the bridal couple strays,
Where whirl the vigorous dancers in the myriad candles' blaze,
There higher swells the bodice of many a youthful dame,
While hearts under knightly doublets heave with a kindred flame.

But who is he, good fellow, in yonder corner found,
With Rhenish wines, and French wines, and goblets heap'd around;
With a crowd of gapers listening, as if marvels would never cease,
As they paint the wolf in Vienna, a-preaching to the geese?

His eye is soft and radiant, his lip just curl'd with scorn,
His brow is old and wrinkled, but his cheek wears the flush of morn;
He is Conrad von der Rosen, by the courtiers call'd a fool,
Yet the wise man feels he's wiser for a lesson in his school.

And as he saw the bridegroom approaching with the bride,
He raised two brimming goblets, stood up, and thus he cried:
"Hail to Burgundy and Austria! Hail, noble pair, to you!
For near is what was distant, and single what was two!

"Thus we behold two rainbows born of a single sun,
Where river flows to river, forsooth, the stream is one;
What are two flowers apart are a nosegay in society,
And two sorts of wine in the head give rise to one inebriety!"

V. THE NUPTIALS.

AT Bruges in the minster, on columns and on shrines,
From thousand candelabras, a wondrous radiance shines:
Bands of priests in splendid garments defile beneath its arches,
While without a lordly company to the Cathedral marches.

Borne loftily before them the double banner streams,
Where Burgundy's gold lily-wreath on Austria's purple gleams:
Very strong is the alliance of such people and such lands,
But the wreath to which the lovers turn twines firmer, stronger bands.

From seventy lands, a herald bears the banner of each land,
Of knights in shining armour, a noble blooming band;
They ride in earnest silence, by God's breath circled round,
While the horses stamp and neigh and the rattling arms resound.

White as the foam of fountains, many hundred horses prance,
On helmets, and on lances, the green sprays float and dance;
Many hundred armours glisten, as the snow in moonlight gleams,
And harp-strings make a music, like the ripples of the streams.

If a sea-gull, sweeping over it, in the air should chance to be,
He would dive to bathe his plumage in such a silver sea;
The nightingale whose threnody from yon balcony trills,
Would think the space beneath him a grove of laurel fills.

Three wagon-loads of mountebanks appear in the procession,
They are all as prim and modest as monks at a confession:
Even Conrad their good master no tricks or pranks can play,
For the fool it is a festival, he need not fool to-day.

Thou, the master of this pageant and this merry mummery,
Wouldst bid to the feast the outcasts who in the prisons be;
That they may see God's daylight, that they may breathe God's
breath,
Their grave doors thou wouldst open, and break the chains of Death.

See how the bridal coronets with precious brilliants glow,
But the eyes of the bridal couple a purer radiance show;
How still the lips, yet speaking with such emphasis and grace,
He recks not of their ornaments who looks into their face.

In the house of God his blessing the grey-hair'd Bishop spake,
And the plain gold rings of wedlock, bride and bridegroom give and take;
Then snapp'd the ring of one of them—it boded nothing good—
And the light of an acolyte went out who at the altar stood.

With myriad stars, the canopy of heaven was lit that night,
But the lights by far outnumber'd them that made all Bruges bright,
And if you cannot read the scroll that God wrote in the sky,
You may read on the town-house written a plain transparency:

"In marriage, happy Austria, not in arms thy fortunes be,[5]
Mars gives to others kingdoms that Venus gives to thee."
Max and Mary's names thereunder inscribed in colour'd light,
Did they see them? History tells not if they saw the scroll that night.

The Eagle and the Lily.°

I. THE SUMMONS.

HILE here our time we're wasting in tournament and dance,
They drink our wine in Burgundy, these easy sons of France;
While here our ears we tickle with telling tales and singing,
There the frequent crack of the musket sets many an ear a-ringing.

"A fool, that on his death-bed would twine a nuptial wreath!
Who would not tear the plaything from the bony hand of Death?
'Mid shouts and shrieks for succour, and the fire-bell's alarm,
By his burning house what simpleton would cry—How fine and warm!

"Then up, ye Lords and Nobles! dance to the trumpets bray,
Win in fight a fresher garland! throw these wither'd wreaths away.
Up! and your steps to the marches right speedily incline,
And with your French Amphytrions invite yourselves to dine."

Thus Max's speech resounded through the high and splendid hall,
A peal of approbation went forth from the nobles all;
And, hark! below from the court-yard, outringing loud and clear,
Above the shouts of the revellers, the neigh of a horse they hear.

All eyes are turn'd to the window whence comes this sudden sound,
And a white steed stood thereunder to a marble column bound;
"A noble beast, by the heavens! prithee tell me from what stall?"
Their heads the courtiers shook then, and shrugg'd their shoulders all.

His neck, how proudly arching! How full of fire his eye!
A glossy skin, and spotless as the blue of a spring-tide sky!
His golden tassell'd trappings with a tinkle-tinkle sound,
As with hoof superbly pawing he stamps upon the ground.

The beast his purple saddle-cloth wears proudly as a king,
"Ha! ha! behold a billet-doux—a very funny thing!
Under the tail suspended, a milk-white missive see,
Now, somebody, run down there and find what that may be."

One lifts the tail and cautiously he takes the letter thence,
Writ of the following tenor or in the following sense :
" We, Louis, of France the eleventh, Navarre et cætera,
King by the grace of God, and Duke of Burgundia."

" Ah, fastens our Cousin his mandate in such a place? Indeed—
The jest is really a merry one—continue, I pray, to read."
Max takes the banter laughingly, but rage burns in his eye,
Thus laughs the distant welkin, where the forkéd lightnings lie.

" To our well-belovéd cousin, and Austria's arch-duke,
They say you mean to visit us, and we wish on you to look :
We therefore send this horse to you, and hope the nag will suit,
We should be very sorry if you came so far on foot.

" Your stingy papa,[7] for your schooling with his money would not part,
So I'm sending you schoolmasters in the military art ;
The noble art to acquire befits a knight like you ;
Honour to God and the Virgin! and till you arrive, adieu!"

Then spake the Hapsburg's scion: " You may enjoy the jeer,
This King knows how right deftly to give a box on the ear;
We are as a guest invited—then quick, to horse! to horse!
Good stipends to good masters—in our education course!"

II. THE CAMP.

FORSOOTH, a peaceful city! the beautiful St. Omer;
Here the young green of the meadows, the silver river there;
Near by, a lake like a mirror, where emerald islands swim,
Where herds of cattle drifting crop the grass at the water's brim.

The Abbey of St. Andomar in polish'd marble drest,
Looks like the Angel of Peace on the land that it has blest.
The little word, War! oh, never was it heard on her fertile plains,
And writ in her cloister's chronicle only half the word remains.

Here seem'd peace and content from the earliest time to dwell;
Was ever heard sound of iron, it was only the tinkling bell;
Did any one cry for succour, 'twas at most but a sheep astray,
Was any one angry, 'twas only a priest in a pastoral way.

But now a vast encampment from lake to abbey extends,
Where the warrior's shout outsoundeth the bells with which it blends,
Outshining the waves, the canvas of the white pavilions gleams,
And the minster with its pinnacles a spirit of vengeance seems.

Pavilion on pavilion, Max's camp is standing there,
And many-coloured banners are fluttering in the air;
High over all, the German Imperial Eagle flies,
And gathers under its pinions native hearts and brave allies.

Every race of Flemish speech in the varied ranks appears,
Even Albion's archers mingle with the Austrian cuirassiers;
And many for whom on the Ister the tears of maidens flow,
Divers tongues, and divers standards—one heart, one head, one foe!

Believe me, a strange encampment, and not the cradle of fight!
No countenance dark or sullen—but every visage is bright;
Is it the wondrous power of the soil devoted to peace?
Of the tranquil times that are vanish'd, will the influence never
cease?

When the martial trumpet sounds, it sounds like the call to a dance,
And the eye of many a knight, once bright with a merry glance,
Is dimm'd with tears, and he sees in the helmet a faded bouquet,
If he hum a war-song it changeth forthwith to a bridal lay.

And Max himself when he wander'd through the camp in musing
mood,
Look'd askance as if at his elbow another figure stood;

Words to his lips came often when sole and apart he roved,
And once, when his fool was beside him, he murmur'd, "My beloved!"

And when in his pavilion he rests in arms at night,
And thinks to see a vision of burning, blood, and fight,—
Approaches a glorified being, and seems by him to stand,
And the green palms of peace waves over him with white hand.

III. THE DUEL.

EVERY morning when the sun through the clouds broke golden-red,
And the glow of purple roses on tower and hill-top shed,
On the field of the encampment where the German army lay,
From tent to tent, well-mounted, a French knight spurr'd his way.

He twisted his mustachio with a sneer of scornful pride,
At every tent he halted, and smote his shield and cried,
"Come out, some gallant German, who will his manhood prove,
To the honour of his country, and the honour of his love."

They let him carry it on so—such is not the German way!
They stay'd in their tents pretending not to hear what he had to
say:
Then in haughty self-sufficiency, away the mad knight sprang,
And his yell of scorn in the distance like a thousand devils rang.

And again flamed in the Orient the purple light of morn,
And again the earth rejoicing, a golden day was born;
And again the Frenchman starting on his diurnal tramp,
Clad cap-à-pie in armour made the circuit of the camp.

A red plume waved defiantly over his haughty head,
The feathers that floated over the front of his horse were red,
Over his stalwart shoulders a red war-cloak he wore,
And a purple-red caparison his snorting charger bore.

He wore a scarf of scarlet, as red as the blood of youth,
The colour himself had chosen and it suited him well, forsooth;
Far into France from the sea-side, the land with his fame had rung,
And as "the mighty Cut-throat" he was known by old and young.

And his bearded lip he twisted again with scornful pride,
Look'd on the German quarters, and rapp'd his shield and cried:
"Come out, some valiant German, who in arms with me will stand
For the honour of his lady, for the honour of his land."

Like the full moon, when suddenly from a cloud it issues bright,
On a swift palfry riding, appear'd a gallant knight;
The gallant knight in a vizor his countenance had mask'd,
"Who is he?" in astonishment, both French and Germans ask'd.

Over his helmet floating no graceful feather streams,
Upon his shining hanger a single gold star gleams:
Is it Love's purple planet, that, alas! so soon declines,
Is it Hope's star, pale and tranquil, that ever smiling shines?

There flows over his shoulders no jaunty martial vest,
Rough is the iron harness that sheathes his manly breast;
A scarf of silk and silver athwart his breast-plate sways,
Where is writ in golden letters, "God's be the glory and praise!"

As if he might be vanquish'd, rides modestly the knight,
Yet all may see his purpose is to conquer in the fight;
No gold and no embossment on his iron buckler weighs,
Yet flames in his heart right loyally "God's be the glory and praise!"

Now German crowds and Flemish the combatants surround,
Now flutter all the banners and all the trumpets sound;
Then met in fierce encounter, each on the other springs,
Then dash the shields together, and spear on háuberk rings.

Behold, the spears are splintered! See, sword on sword descend!
Now, thinks the Gallic Cut-throat, the struggle soon must end;
Under the blows of his good sword crack'd many an iron band,
Till burst the helm of his enemy and tumbled in the sand.

See down his neck unrolling his hair in a golden stream;
Blue as the dome of heaven two clear eyes smiling beam;
There glances also a sunlight so blinding in its rays,
That of such a sun the Frenchman cannot endure the blaze.

He starts and stares aghast, while the sword drops from his hand,
As if he saw an Avenger come from the spirit land:
But the German sword descending its mighty blows resound,
His senses swim, the Cut-throat falls staggering to the ground.

Then exultingly the Germans raise the shout from man to man,
"Hail, angel of German vengeance! Hail, Maximilian!"
But the weapon stain'd with bloodshed he gladly tosses away,
And crying, "To God be the glory!" sinks on his knee to pray.

IV. THE DECISION.

(7 *August*, 1479.)

THERE is a Northland country, where for months the
twilight lies;
Where day and night together divide the dusky skies;
It is both, and yet is neither—with this war in the same way,
Two armies are defeated, and neither wins the day.

And if all the dead it slaughter'd were in one coffin laid,
Fell its woods, and such a coffin from Ardennes could not be made;
Could you gather in one ocean all the tears it caused to flow,
There Love the inconsolable might haply drown his woe.

See you yon shining ramparts? Peal on peal the thunder cracks.
Those are the walls of Terouenne, and the batteries of Max:
And see you the shine of weapons, that gleam where the distant
blue is?
There Crèvecœur is commanding the veteran troops of Louis.

Before the walls of Terouenne there lies a verdant lea,
Reaching as far as Guinegate, and level as the sea ;
There rides Max deeply pondering, his eye sweeps swift around,
" Wide enough for defeat and triumph ! A noble battle-ground !

" I can fancy myself a grave-digger in these death-dealing days ;
For before the fight the general, who the field of fight surveys,
And the sexton when he shovels, have the same thought in their
head ;
' I must see if there is room enough for burying my dead.'

" Yet see there France's banners in the distant azure blow,
Up ! let us sound the onset, and quick engage the foe :
Why here in dull entrenchments shall we sit before the walls,
When there to wreaths of victory the voice of Glory calls ?"

Max bends in supplication, the embattled warriors kneel,
The glow of a golden sunlight breaks on their coats of steel ;
Like the beams from man's heart springing, when stricken by
Faith's rod,
Like the beams of grace descending from the guardian eye of God.

The beating of drums and the war-cries ! Then army on army
rush,
And mighty indeed is the meeting, as when mountains on mountains
crush :

Pale Death shouted: "Bravo! bravo!" and outrang the prophetic
chorus
Of the swarthy ravens singing, "Thanks! thanks! for the feast
before us!"

There the roar of thundering mortars, here the hiss of bullets flying,
Here the shouts of drunken victors, there the groans of warriors
dying,
Gnashing teeth and imprecations and the broken voice of prayer,
Here Crèvecœur, "Forward, dastards!" and Max, "Stand,
brothers," there!

And all again is quiet! Clouds of dust in eddies blow,
We hear the clash of weapons, but no one sees his foe:
Save where a gust of wind of the slaughter'd gives a glance,
And shows to the victors' enemy where the hearts of the victors
dance.

The other side waves and totters, the French ranks break and
yield,
Already shouts the German, "Ours is the battle-field!"
The might of France is crumbled, her hosts disorder'd fly,
And with the gather'd lily the eagle seeks the sky.

Max thinks when he rides at evening through the devastated plain,
"Is not the battle a tempest that scatters death in its train?
There's a rush of two clouds together, there's lightning and thunder
and sleet,
The hail rustles down with havoc, and the fields stand reft of their
wheat.

"It may be clear'd and brighten'd, the sky's celestial blue,
There may shimmer on the foliage a fresher diamond dew;
Peace in the brightest colours her bow in the heavens may form,
But she cannot revive the harvest that perish'd in the storm."

V. VOICES.

IN the market-place of Ghent are the captured flags dis-
play'd,
Under triumphal arches rides the dashing cavalcade;
Before the royal palace the pageant train defiles,
In the midst a handsome warrior on a blooming infant smiles.

His spring-flowers to the gardener do not give so much delight,
As to the happy father the infant's visage bright;
As she seeks her virgin image in the eye of her nursling boy,
And in that clear fount finds it,—the mother is rapt with joy!

Oh, Max, how bright the sunshine of fortune and renown!
Thy child hangs on thy lips[8] and thy head wears the laurel crown;
Many true friends surround thee, the loved one leans on thy breast,
Whom does the sun in his circuit behold more richly blest?

Triumphal feasts and jubilees are held on every hand,
And pæans ring from the centre to the borders of the land—
In the castles and the cities—through Hainault and Burgundy,
Behold the lilies trampled, the eagle flutters free!

Then mutters France's Louis half laughing at his jibe,—
"This eagle's a bird of passage, of a very special tribe;
For while the storks and swallows return to their homes in spring,
The eagle remains till autumn abroad upon the wing."

And Max in Ghent at the banquet says in a merry way,
"What wonder, that, in autumn, when the sunshine makes short stay,
The roses and carnations and tulips lose their glow?
It is natural enough then that the lilies should not blow."

Love's Parting.[9]

(1482.)

I. THE HERON CHASE.

WHEN spring again encircles the earth in her genial embrace,
There rides from the gates of Bruges a party for the chase;
Full many handsome falconers on shapely coursers ride,
And withal the beautiful duchess by her loving husband's side.

On her arm there sat a falcon. From the whiteness of his vest
At court they gave him the title of Dominican in jest:
His head a black hood covered, a silver collar he wore,
Which the inscription "Upwards," in golden letters bore.

A desolate heath outstretches, of bloom and verdure bare,
Where only thorn bushes flourish, in patches here and there:
On the left the bath of the herons, a little fish-pond, lay,
And here they wash their plumage, and thus their haunt betray.

There's a rush into the water, and a scream from the crackling reeds,
And a flight of frightened herons to the right and left succeeds,
The vigorous falcons circling from the wrists of the hunters fly,
And mount, as the thoughts of man mount, to the azure of the sky.

And the eye of every hunter follows his falcon's flight,
As in its aerial circles it sweeps to the left and the right;
Alertly in all directions the eager hunters move,
The earth beneath them trembles, clouds of dust are whirled above.

But see with mane all streaming there runs a riderless horse,
How it snorts! how with fright it quivers! how it springs on its tangled course!
Hold on! Seize the reins of the runaway! How and where fell the rider? Alas!
There lies the beautiful duchess—and there is the blood stain'd grass!

She leans her pallid countenance upon her husband's breast,
As white as the evening cloud is when the last flush fades in the west;

Ah! how from life's genial sources the precious red streams start!
Alas! how richly blossoms the crimson rose of her heart!

A pair of weeping children,[10] a sister and a brother,
Bend like twin angels, tenderly, over the pale, dead mother;
So bend twin dewy rosebuds on the same parent spray,
Over the mother flower that storm-stricken fades away!

His head downcast in sadness, where her blood the green turf stains,
By her side the white Dominican with mournful look remains;
Would you know his little motto? he had been her own apt scholar,
"Upwards!" in golden letters still gleams upon his collar.

II. CONJURATION.

HE night is dark and starless, the hour is waxing late,
When the janitor at Spannheim opens the cloister gate;
And a man, in a cloak enveloped, the threshold passes o'er,
Treads through the crossways silently, and knocks at the abbot's door.

In whatever place Sir Trittheim," the abbot, might appear,
The laity uncover'd their heads in reverend fear;
Before him in mute obeisance the ancient doctors bow'd,
And beneath the monkish habit full many a heart beat loud.

Immersed in prayer, the holy man was burning the midnight oil,
And reading in books of wisdom, and working in studious toil;
When his cell the stranger enter'd, whose step the silence broke,
Young in form but grey in sorrows, and thus the stranger spoke:

"Most reverend sir, a monarch in tears before you stands,
But lately rich in love as in honours and in lands,
Yet now for ever vassal! Grief is his paramount lord,
Heavy rests on head and shoulders the tyrant's hand abhorr'd.

"The crown remains mine only; with love, alas! I part,
And the sharp spikes of the diadem now penetrate my heart;
There in the world of spirits, you wander a friendly guest,
Oh, father, then call my loved one down from the home of the blest!"

With sympathy and compassion the eye of the abbot glows,
His sable beard luxuriantly over his vestment flows,

He rises full of dignity, with an aspect of command,
Surveys his guest intently and takes him by the hand.

Through the still walks of the cloisters, where Echo only wakes,—
Out in the night—the stranger his course with the abbot takes;
Like a pilgrim in the catacombs who wanders from his way,
Damp airs his torch extinguish—he wanders in dismay.

In sombre shrouds the mountains invest their giant forms,
Like an old witch bewailing, the North Wind shrieks and storms;
There's a roar of billows and branches which yet no eye can see,
And many a deer all bloody bounds back from the old oak-tree.

And now they both stand silent. The abbot kneels to pray,
There's a flame in the heavens a moment, and it instantly dies away;
And lo! in the ebon background of the moonless, starless night,
Two lustrous sceptres sparkle with a blaze of golden light.

"Creation and Destruction! My prince, your choice I crave,
On golden shafts uplifted—here life and there the grave!
With that his human kindred the wise man wisely rules,
While this to lash their people is a scourge in the hand of fools.

"A simple staff one shineth — which mortal weakness props;
The other is sharp as a dagger, and its rubies are blood-drops;
What seem pure liquid diamonds are only petrified tears,
While deeply impressed on the handle the grip of a tyrant appears.

"In the soil where the seeds of the ages ripen to blossom and fruit,
This may serve as a pillar of shame, a trunk from a wither'd root;
The other is green as a palm-tree, exempt from meridian glows,
With a crown of the richest foliage, whereunder you softly repose."

Thus speaks the austere abbot. The sceptres fade away,
And for a moment the darkness holds undivided sway;
When a star uprises suddenly, it is very large and light,
And from its depth a countenance smiles radiantly bright.

"Behold! serene and tearless, she shines upon the earth,
With pain and tears she parted at her celestial birth:
As the white rose and the cypress in funeral beauty bloom,
While smiling from the heavens she looks upon her tomb.

"A great work rests upon thee! The ruler's career is to do!
From deeds erect her monument! Forthwith thy mission pursue!
To lift its glance to the sun can an eye wet with weeping dare?
Can a hand that trembles or falters with honour the sceptre bear?

"To mitigate your sorrows, to strengthen you for duty,
To kindle a noble ardour for works of worth and beauty,
These are the spells and charms with which God doth the priest invest,
Be strong, my prince, be prudent, and thy empire will be blest."

Thus solemnly the priest; the prince received the council well,
Press'd his hand, and into the darkness pass'd from the abbot's cell.
He reached the crown thereafter, and who has better worn it?
He boldly grasp'd the sceptre, and who has better borne it?

The flowers all weep and glisten in the flush of early morn,
The fountains gush when the garlands of spring their banks adorn;
And Max, ever thereafter, in his days of power and fame,
Cover'd his eyes and his tears at the whisper of Mary's name.

Max and Flanders.

I. THE AWAKING.

HE royal lion slumbering, mute on a tombstone lay,
Gaily frisking about him the mice held holiday;
But softly, ye merry companions, or you'll find yourselves in the wrong,
Pray do not venture too boldly, for lions do not sleep long.

Even lions are weak in slumber—so lion, sleep no more;
From the woods of Ardennes[12] already snorts the ferocious boar;
Who tramples thy blooming gardens, and thy fruitful harvest husks,
And on the trunks of the poplars sharpens his bloody tusks.

Wake! do you not wake from your slumber at the sound of Roland's bell?[13]
Hark! how at Ghent it threatens—and wakes Liège and Bruges as well!

'Tis the signal of fire—Rebellion is kindling throughout the land,
And the spark by the treacherous Frenchman to a raging flame
is fann'd.[14]

Wake up, O Max! rush onward and a bloody harvest reap,
If French craft and Flemish treason fail to rouse thee from thy
sleep,
Then bray it in thine ears with the trumpet's shrillest sound,
Wake up, thy son is a captive, thy son is a prisoner bound![15]

Awake is the royal lion, he reaches the goal with a bound;
How his mane glows! Where he rages, how life grows pale around!
The mighty boar knows already the grip of the lion is sure,
And will with his own black blood the crops of the field manure.

So loud, Ghent, as the mortars, thy Roland thunders not,
Thou hast thrust thy fingers, Frenchman, in a bonfire flaming hot,
And, mutinous men of Flanders! the eagle your fury mocks,
And has borne his young through the tempest to his eyrie on the
rocks!

II. MAX BEFORE DENDERMONDE.

WITH a smiling aspect, Dendermond' salutes the traveller's eyes,
When bathed in evening sunshine the stately fortress lies,
On thee, Max, it looks frowningly, for Rebellion rules the hour,
And plants her lawless standard on battlement and tower.

The Abbot of Dendermonde sat with his monks to dine,
And glass on glass he emptied of the precious cloister wine;
"Now brothers in Christ, surgamus! sit not in idle talk,
It behoves us to be industrious, so let us go out for a walk."

In Dendermond' the Abbess, and her nuns in rapt devotion
Read the legend of St. Abelard, with the tenderest emotion;
"Let us sing, this pleasant evening, abroad in the open air,—
To interrupt our psalmody, no dogs are howling there."

The nuns then, and the friars with breviaries and beads,
Saunter out by the town-gates into the verdant meads;
"O Christ!" the nuns are singing, "thou bridegroom true and tried!"
The monks are sighing, "Mary, O come thou charming bride!"

And as two and two together through the greenwood took their way,
Came a rustling in the branches and a voice like thunder—
"Stay!"
Then through the tangled thicket a band of warriors break,
The cheeks of the nuns grow paler, and the knees of the friars shake.

Impetuous through the brushwood plunges a panting horse,
Its rider of gallant bearing, in the midst of a mailéd force,
He cries, "In God's name, welcome—you have wander'd out of
your way,
God bless you, Lady Abbess, Sir Abbot too, good day!"

"Max of Austria salutes you. I myself am in the field,
But for your accommodation my tents I'll gladly yield,
Indeed, I keep spare table, some poor men keep a richer,—
But with sundry smoking-platters and many a brimming pitcher.

"Things are not to my liking, and I would fain amuse me,
And your aid in a harmless mummery I'm sure you'll not refuse me,
So I beg you'll lend us cowls and hoods and veils, for an excursion,
In a sort of masquerading, that I've plann'd for our diversion."

The friars wag their beards, and the cheeks of the nuns are a-glow,
And low they mutter in chorus, "Lord, help us in our woe!"

Then Max gives the word to his warriors, "On with the veil and the
gown!
On with the cowl and the cassock, and hurry into the town!"

"To fit in the cowl of the Abbot, my grey beard will hardly fail,
And you, my merry friend, Conrad, shall wear the Abbess's veil;
The enterprise is a foolish one, and therefore in your way,
God willing, we'll meet in Dendermond' before the break of day."

Veil'd and cowl'd they stand already, nuns and friars in a row,
How splendidly round Conrad the robes of the Abbess flow!
And as the beautiful Abbess hung the veil about his face,
He thought as many another fool would be sure to think in his place.

Upon the walls at Dendermond' a sentinel keeps watch,
Who leans on his spear in the moonlight and trolls a merry catch,
"A monk and so a monkey, the jingle's good and fine,
A monk and so a monkey, both love a wench and wine."

"Ho, infidel, may the thunder scald thy polluted throat!
Is that, forsooth, thine orison? Shut up that slanderous note."
Thus the shout of the self-made Abbot at Dendermond's gateway
rung,
The while his nuns and novices in impatient chorus sung.

"Pardon, Sir Abbot, but surely this is a marvellous case,
The Abbot swears like a pirate, and the Abbess speaks in bass."
Thus muttering, half-bewilder'd, the watchman shakes his pate,
Then creak the brazen hinges, and open stands the gate.

"Should you like your fee for admission? You sing uncommonly well,
And a notable song I'll teach you; it does not ring clear as a bell,
But it's proper and pious, and instantly carries you heavenward, ho!"
Thus shouted the Lady Abbess, and followed the word with a blow.

Ha! what a clatter of swords! What a rush in the crowded street!
What a terrible howl of confusion, when alarm-bells the field-cry meet!
Never struck nuns, it is certain, such ponderous blows as to-night,
Never sent monks such a number of souls on their heavenward flight.

The trumpet brays at the gateway, there's a rattle of drums without,
There's a tramping and stamping of horses, and listen to Max's shout!
"Welcome to Dendermonde! Carry your banners high,
And from the tops of the turrets proclaim your victory."

In the morn the victor summons the leaders of the rising,
"Welcome; this early meeting is to both no doubt surprising;
But mark as a priest I come here, not to avenge my wrongs,
Peace and pardon speak the office which to the priest belongs."

III. A GOOD ENDING.

WHY sounds the blast of the trumpet? That is Frederick Von Horn:
"My prince, I have tamed at its grimmest the Wild Boar's rage and scorn."
Who approaches with flying colours? Of Nassau, Sir Engelbright.
"My prince, I took these banners from the Frenchman in the fight."

Hark to the bells with their chimings that from the steeples ring,
See Ghent the keys of the city on velvet cushion bring:
Oh, Max, why gladdens thy visage, why trembles thy vigorous arm?
Thy son hangs again on thy bosom, and clings to thy lips so warm!

Joy! joy! From his eyes how richly the fountain of gladness springs,
How fondly he kisses the darling, how fondly he hugs him and swings!

And what is the saintly shimmer that on thy forehead appears?
Is it a garland of pearls, boy, or is it thy father's tears?

"A fool ought not to be weeping,"—thinks Conrad, who stands hard by,
"A fool ought not to be weeping,"—but the briny drop gleams in his eye:
"And if ever it happen the singer tells our story in future years,
The ninny'll not fail in his ditty for lack of pathos and tears!"

Maximilian, Roman King.[17]

(1486.)

A GOLDEN crown on the worn-out head is a heavy load
for me—
My strong son, Max, the burden will be easier for
thee!
The sceptre I wield tremblingly will rest firm in thy hand,"—
The old emperor was thinking so, and so thought all the land.

'Tis Max's coronation. At Aix, in the minster's nave,
Flash the mitres and the helmets, the silks and velvets wave ;
On his brow the holy ointment inaugurates his reign,
And with steady grasp he handles the sword of Charlemagne.

Behold Cologne's grey bishop before the altar stand,
Like a true friend and cordial, Old Age now shakes his hand,
Yet firmly and without trembling he places the jewelled crown,
He knows that on a better head priest never set it down.

The organ has ceased its pealing. There follows a collation,
Where sit the lords and princes—to crown the coronation!
From urns of silver gurgle streams of refreshing wine,
And blue clouds are curling upwards where the golden platters
shine.

The Palatine swung the goblet and rose to a taunting toast:
"To old father Rhine, a bumper! for who, my Lords, will boast,
That he can show a jewel, in all his broad domain,
Which, like my purple vintage, can fire the heart and brain?"

Then the princes in succession praise the kingdom and the throne,
The old Emperor praises Austria, and each one lauds his own;
To the Bishop his great minster the world's great marvel seems;
And Louis of Bavaria lauds her meadows and blue streams.

From Saxony, Sir Albert says, "In sooth, my treasures shine
As ores of gold and iron, in the dark shafts of the mine;
The gold our women teaches to be refined and pure,
The iron makes our manhood reliable and sure."

Then spake the Wurtemberger, Count Everhard of the Beard,
"Such jewels in my country have never yet appear'd;
But there's not in all its borders a wilderness so deep,
That, on a subject's pillow there, I could not safely sleep."

Max once in such a contest would have had a word to say;
But now the dark earth buries all the brightness of his day:
In melancholy silence a moment lost he stands.
In his own, then, gently presses the Wurtemberger's hands.

Throne and Tripod.[18]

(February to May, 1488.)

I. THE GUILDS.

THE guild-masters of Bruges sat by cards, and wine, and song,
The sailor, smith, and dyer had sat there all day long;
And Coppenoll, the cobbler, from Ghent, was present too;
He bawled in council the loudest, and made the meanest shoe.

The cobbler spake: "My masters, know ye the news to-night?
The king is coming to Candlemas, God grant, Let there be light!"
At this the dyer stealthily peeps in the cards of the smith,
Meanwhile of a fine old carol he is merrily humming the pith.

"A little king there once was—a marmot, you may say—
Of work he had his hands full, for he slept both night and day;
At night, because 'tis the fashion in life to sleep by night,
And by day because his slumbers had fatigued and tired him quite."

Then spake the smith:—"This Max here is made of the right stuff;
He was always a gallant fellow, and I like him well enough:
But all the lords his courtiers with hoofs of iron prance,
And on the corns of the people they love to tread and dance."

With a sly chuckle the cobbler the smith on the shoulders hit,
"I should like to make their boots for them—I'd give them a tight fit."
Then the dyer slapped on the table and tossed off his stoup of wine,
And roar'd—"The King of Clubs, bravo! the Knave of Diamonds is mine."

Then the sailor dash'd in anger his cards upon the floor,—
"A god-forsaken life it is you people live on shore;
Damme! It always happens the knave is trumped by the king:—"
All spring up in confusion, stools tumble, and glasses ring.

Then cried the smith, "A sceptre, forsooth, is a sorry thing;
For me such work would not answer, but 'twill do well enough for a king:"

Then the dyer—"At home there lie mouldering many red rags of
my own,
Which, hung on the stool of the cobbler, would make it as fine as a
throne."

Stood Coppenoll the cobbler, who gravely shook his head,
Oppressed with thought, and muttering, thus to himself he said,—
"Respublica but recently has rubbed a hole in her shoe,
And Master Coppenoll reckons the cobbling's for him to do.

"These kings—who gives the sceptre, gentlemen, into their hands?
He who reigns in the heavens. He also created their lands.
The Netherlands we have created, by our own labour and pains,
So the right of choosing our master in our own hands remains."

"Bravo! thou gallant master! thou shalt our leader be."
So the others fall into chorus, and all shout clamorously;
Out of the doors they tumble, the towers and steeples gain,
And set the bells ringing the tocsin, and howl like a hurricane.

In the market-place already the guilds their banners flaunted,
And all the guild companions under them stood undaunted,
Then first began in a whisper, then louder and louder to roll,
From the mouth of the people and head-men, "Our leader be
Coppenoll!"

In the streets and squares there's a shouting, there's a howl, and a
roar, and a rush,
They ply the hammer and pick-axe, and the kingly columns crush;
Many the sceptres of iron, and the crowns that yield to their blows,
With many a king's wooden noddle, and many a stony lord's nose.

II. THE WARNING.

LIES yet on the plains of Flanders the winter's mantle of
snow,
Where glancing like trimmings of silver, the lagoons in
the sunshine glow;
In the far blue the pinnacles of Bruges shimmer bright,
Like stars of gold embroider'd on a mantle's silver white.

Deep buried in their jerkins a band of riders go,
With frost their beards empearlèd, through the crackling fields of
snow;
By the side of King Max Conrad breaks many a merry jest,
While his eyes with the sleet are weeping, his heart laughs in his
breast.

The king with emotion pointed to the fields which before him lay;
"With what a voice it speaks there—Behold, what man's Art may!
Thou liest as array'd for a bridal, oh, Flanders, my lovely land!
In a white robe of slumber, girt with a silver band."

Then Conrad,—"Yes, yes, truly,—like a faded beauty that;
There's not an attractive prominence, but all is smooth and flat;
Somewhat loose in the girdle, dressed up by night and day,
And yet thou findest a lover! A proof of what Art may!

"All these ponds and these waters may serve as looking-glasses,
(They need any number of mirrors, these antiquated lasses)—
They're of small dimensions luckily, and their shine is somewhat
dull,
Thou wouldst certainly be frighten'd, if thou saw'st thyself in full."

"And in thy speech thou stammerest, as strangers in Germany
speak,
Their own tongue they have forgotten, and in German they are
weak;
As a good housewife, thou sweepest thy barn and thy granary oft,
And, in order not to soil them, thou pilest no corn in the loft.

"And as to thy cellar, oh, Murder! like a washy drinking song,
Where the wine is hard to discover, the water is so strong;

My lord and king, I imagine, you had better let her alone;
They say that of him she embraces, she spares neither nerve nor
bone.

"Think, now, of the old giant—the story you know full well,
And of what to him with the hussy in Philistia befell;
She stole from him in the night-time his beautiful golden hair;
It seems to me, Miss Flandria neither head nor locks will spare."

"A truce to your evil surmises!" Max with impatience said:
"Of princes who have sworn fealty, one cannot be afraid;
For their word and faith like beacons beam with unfading light,
And Truth at their golden portals stands sentry day and night."

"No crown ever pressed my forehead—I'm a bachelor and a fool,
And little of such high knowledge did I ever learn at school;
But, in sooth, I think it much better to be a fool on the wing,
Than to be a wise man in prison, though the wise man were a king.

"Item, remember, the proverb that I'm sure you've often heard,—
Let the continence of a friar with the sense of a lover be stirr'd,
Mix in a youngster's modesty, with a sauce of Flemish truth,
Give the whole to a mite for his breakfast, and you'll sharpen his
hungry tooth.

"Indeed I do not much fancy your comrade in jail to be,
Therefore, my farewell I tender—but think of my warning and me;
Prithee, Max, to truth's voice listen, before it shall be too late,
As once again I implore you not to enter Bruges' gate."

So speaks the Von der Rosen. Max sternly shakes his head,
Though as the gate he enters, he thrills with a secret dread;
But the presage he quickly suppresses, and enters the palace of state,
While Conrad is off at a tangent, and out by another gate.

III. THE KRANENBURG.

SIR COPPENOLL in the council house till his fingers were tired wrote,
Then said to his boy in waiting, "Come, comrade, take this note
To Mister Maximilian, take it with my salute":
The lad receives the missive, and bows in reverence mute.

"Since two suns in the firmament cannot together shine,
And when one reaches the zenith, the other must needs decline,
And, as when the eagle's at liberty, he will rob as eagles do,
Therefore the people of Bruges have furnish'd a cage for you."

This was the text of the letter which Max now laughing read,
On which, display'd like a crawfish, the seal of the guilds was spread,
And Coppenoll's name thereunder in crooked flourishes stands,
By dingy clouds surrounded, the marks of the cobbler's hands.

"We're now in the midst of the Carnival, so I enjoy your joke"—
Thus spake Max to the messenger, and thus aside he spoke;
"Place in your heavens no lamplight, for in sooth I'll not engage
That the eagle you hold captive does not break the bars of his cage."

Thence went he to the Kranenburg, a prison for the nonce,
Though here the roots of the Orient a shopman vended once,
Here amber and myrrh and balsam their perfumes still dispense,
And the young king learns to value the odour of frankincense.

Now the people reign at Bruges. The trades are at a stand.
The tanner gives to governing the days when once he tann'd.
The shopkeeper wields the sceptre who once the yardstick bore—
The sexton only shovels and does business as before.

IV. THE TRUE SERVANT.

BURIED once in meditation Max paced his prison floor,
When, with gentle step approaching, some one knock'd upon the door;
His face in a brown cowl muffled, his back bow'd down and crook'd,
A monk stood in the chamber, and about with caution look'd.

" God is a grinder of eye-glasses, he has glasses white and clear,
We men are the buyers, to one of us the glasses seem dull and blear,
Another they nip in the nose, to the third they are just the thing,
I fancy I'll suit you exactly, for Hope's green glasses I bring."

"Make it short, good father—but, hark ye, and pardon the suggestion,
This cowl suits your rogue's visage—it don't admit of question—
As smiling spring suits winter, as laughing suits with crying,
Like a rose of the fullest blossom in the fringe of a priest's hood lying."

" You divine your Von der Rosen, my dearest Max, is here—
Your Conrad to deliver you in monkish garb stands near ;—"
" Welcome, my lad, thrice welcome, your heart with true blood swells,
But tell me why for a cowl you have left the cap and bells ?"

Then to the neck of his monarch the joyful Pater flies,
His breast heaves with emotion, and the tears pour from his
eyes;
But his visage fresh and frolicksome in the hood of the friar glows,
As from the dark earth smiling peeps the red Alpine rose.

What wonder? A fool and a friar?—they're certainly made to
match;
If any thing tickles a friar, a fool will be sure to scratch;
They drink from a single goblet, and sit on a single stool,
And now you must follow the friar, since you would not follow
the fool.

"I come to give you freedom. Through the darkness and the cold
I swam the moat, whose waters these prison walls enfold;
The swans flapped their wings with a screeching that could not have
been greater,
If every mother's son of them had been a Flemish traitor.

"In the convent of St. Francis I parley'd with the prior,
Whose healths to your honour daily half a keg of wine require,
And he sent you this cloak as a present, with his greeting and
blessing, of course,
And besides a saddled Frater, and a psalmody singing horse.

"To the emperor at Middleburg now ride without delay,
Thence he sent me with this letter, and I lagged not on the way;
His army to your deliverance impetuously fly,
And now Bavaria, Brandenburg, and Saxony are nigh.

"We'll exchange our coats and dignities,—I'll shave your head quite bare,
And, instead of a golden diadem, you'll take the crown of hair;
How the Flemings will be dumbfoundered, and how I will wriggle with laughter,
When they find the fool in the place of the king they are looking after!"

Then spoke the king, touch'd deeply: "Mark thee, my trusty lad,
From hence be sure I budge not. Thy plan's, in sooth, not bad;
But think'st thou such masquerading becomes the head of a realm?
No! Prudence must spread his canvas, and Piety guide his helm."

"Softly, my dear king, softly. I've a story in point, I think;
One day Prudence and Piety enter'd a tavern to drink;
Piety very politely brimmed two glasses high,
But Prudence, the sly-boots, quietly suck'd both glasses dry.

"My king, you are quite too pious for all this Flemish concern;
Come, take the cowl,—I wager it will serve you no ill turn:

Quick, brother Maximilian, or you'll stay to do much worse;
Up, up! my bold Franciscan: come on—to Horse! to Horse!"

"Fellow, your breath you are wasting," thus Max cried out at last;
"The word that I once have spoken like the rock stands firm and fast;
I've sworn an oath to remain here, it is a monarch's oath,—
Farewell, farewell—deliverance is near at hand for both."

Conrad besought imploringly, but he besought in vain,
Whereon he screw'd his lips up in a serio-comic strain;
And between his teeth he mutter'd: "I' faith, I still may sing,
They will only find a fool here—when they come to look for a king!"

V. SPRING'S MESSAGE.

MAX look'd through the grates of his window, look'd over the walls and the towers,
Where again the Spring was bedecking the fields with its green and its flowers,
When a free little bird familiarly seated himself on the sill,
And look'd on the captive monarch, and warbled a lively trill.

"Thou seest something shine in the distance, and what may the shining be?
It is not Spring's flowers and blossoms, but it's no less welcome to thee:
It is banners and helmets! Thy father, approaching with vengeance swift,
Brings them with him from far to Flanders, to serve as a springtime gift."

"And what is it there uprises, like stalks of wheat from the plain?
Spring surely does not display there her golden spires of grain;
Those stalks are spears, and their blossoms with the promise of blood are red,
On every spike that shines there, hangs a harvest of the dead."

But the captive king divined not if the song was the song of the bird,
Or if from his heart it sounded, the melody he heard;
Yet as a garland of roses falls on the dusky tomb,
So peace and rest descended to light his prison's gloom.

Now storms down the stairs of the tower, into the market place,
Where the guilds stand all collected, Sir Coppenoll, white in the face;
The tower-keeper after him bawling,—"All who have legs now flee!
Countless as flies in summer come the forces of Germany."

"They're not a mile off, and are monsters that would make the bravest shudder,
And all have legs like a horse's, and swords as broad as a rudder,
And beards like a fir-tree's branches, and for us brings every man,
Oh, murder! a great tall gallows—so scamper ye all who can."

Then ran the guild companions, and ran each other down;
And scrambled after their weapons,—here, there, throughout the town;
And first it began to whisper, then louder and louder to roll,
From the mouth of the people and head-men,—"Let us hang Coppenoll!"

VI. THE KING AND THE COBBLER.

"WELCOME, master! but I hardly had known you where you stand,
For since with crown and sceptre you've domineer'd this land,
Your eye-brows are much darker, and your nose is much more ruddy,
And, like the face of a thunder-cloud, your countenance is bloody."

Thus Max joked Master Coppenoll, who, half in his robes of state,
And half in his guild costume enters the prison grate;
The master stands crest-fallen, and like a bellows sighs;
At last he ventures boldly to raise his voice and eyes:—

"Full many a Roman ruler changed the sceptre for the plough,
The noble stately war-horse for the farm-horse and the cow;
For the earthen jug of water changed the goblet of Moselle,
Shall not the Ghenter Coppenoll as the Roman do as well?

"My Prince, my throne and kingdom at your feet I gladly lay,
And as your loyal subject I promise to obey;
So, like the singing-bird, of your cage again be free,
Only cast down forgivingly your glance on such as me."

"If, Sir Master, over winter you imprison birds that sing,
Freedom gives a double sweetness to their carols in the spring;
But if I should sing the song to you that you have taught to me,
You ne'er would sing or listen to such another glee.

"For leg and foot alone is the handicraft you boast,
So kingdoms must be trampled when cobblers rule the roast;
You say you pray for pardon? You are a noble man,
And Max must try to emulate your conduct if he can."

"Thanks, Prince, to my petition pray graciously incline,—
Should you any time hereafter want something in my line,
Don't forget that when I abdicate at Ghent I settle down,
And awl in hand you'll find me, at the sign o' the Broken Crown."

"Well, master, I will promise, but give me first a sample,
Make me a good, long strap, and let it be firm and ample;
Make it of first-rate leather, that will neither stretch nor snap,
If your friends should sometime wish to make a halter of the strap."

The King now left the prison, by Master Coppenoll's side,
"All hail, King Max!" the people in the streets rejoicing cried;
Max cast a look behind him as he left the prison door,
And saw a marble tablet which an inscription bore.

'Twas a pasquinade the rebels had lately graven there,[19]
Max in a loud voice read it, then said with laughing air:
"Why do you write in Latin that only monks can read?
While such a thing, dear people, should be for all indeed!"

VII. WELCOME AND FAREWELL.

MAX on the German camp-field from a foaming courser sprang,
Bright glanced the eyes of the warriors, as their shouts of greeting rang;
The princes, all in their armour, threw themselves on his breast,
How genial the hand of a German in his own with kindness prest!

His trembling arms to embrace him the Emperor extends,
Ha! Frederick, press to your bosom the tenderest of your friends;
Why brush away the tear-drops that from your eyelids roll'd?
Of your tears are you as niggard as they say you are of gold?

Then Max spake: "Grant, my father, and sirs, one prayer of mine,
Let the star of peace on Flanders benevolently shine;
As Violence once, Repentance now traverses the land,
And the sword is wrung by Repentance from Retribution's hand."

" My prince, you are too lenient. for vengeance Germans call,
All for each we here are standing, are standing each for all :"
Thus roar'd Albert the Saxon. His eyes, how they flash'd with ire!
Had the eyes of German princes flamed always with that fire !

" Come on," cried Max, now sadly; " our farewell we must say,
We go to friendly Tyrol, so up, my friends, and away!
Rough is the frock of the peasant, but you hardly need be told,
That right warm hearts are beating beneath its roughest fold.

" On the seeds of my own country my horse shall never tread,
The blood of my own people my sword shall never shed ;
So go your ways, my princes, but the honest burghers spare,
They are the pearls of my diadem, the fairest of the fair."

"Yes, well, my Max, but your purchase of pearls was a costly thing,
I would therefore hang together these pearls upon a string :"
Thus Conrad cried, from the circle of princes popping his head,
Like a simple Forget-me-not peeping from a gorgeous tulip bed.

St. Martin's Wall.[20]

WELCOME, ye hearts of Tyrol, which beat so honestly,
Welcome, ye glaciers of Tyrol, which bear the heavens on high,
Ye dwellings of Fidelity, ye verdant, fragrant vales,
Welcome, ye streams and pastures, freedom and mountain gales!

Who is the daring archer that in hunter's costume stands,
In his hat the beard of the chamois and the cross-bow in his hands;
Whose eye with a youthful ardour, like the eye of a monarch glances,
Whose heart with a quiet rapture in the sport of the hunter dances?

The hunter is Max of Hapsburg, on a lusty chamois chase,
Where scarcely the chamois ventures, he sweeps on the frightful race;

He swings himself upwards, ascending, in his course like an arrow
swift,
How vigorously he clambers over crag and over clift!

Here over heaps of rubble, over deep abysses there,
Now on the ground close creeping, now flying through the air,
And now, hold on! No further! Now is he fast confin'd,
Chasm before, and chasms beside him, and a break-neck wall
behind!

As he soars to the sun, the eagle holds there his earliest rest,
The strength of his wing is broken, and fallen his haughty crest,
If any one thence to the valley a road of stone would lay,
He must quarry all Tyrol and Styria for the pavement of the way.

Max had heard from his nurse in childhood all about St. Martin's
Wall,
Till at the thought a dimness on his vision seemed to fall;
He can see full well already if she painted the scenes with truth,
That he should e'er paint them to others there's little hope now,
forsooth!

His throne the rocky rampart, see the princely scion stand,
His sceptre, the wall-lichen, he grasps with wavering hand,

Above him spreads a vista, so boundlessly display'd,
That before the dizzy prospect his senses faint and fade.

The vale of the Inn before him an emerald carpet spreads,
Streamlet and street drawn through it like a tissue's woven threads;
Far off—colossal mountains to hillocks shrunk lie round,
Each one to Max appearing like an ominous churchyard mound.

With a blast of mighty clangour through his horn for help he calls,
On the air like a peal of thunder, but on air alone it falls;
A little devil titters from a cleft in the nearest rock,—
It falls far short of the valley, his stout horn's fullest shock.

He blows again in his bugle, so loud that it almost breaks,
Ho, ho, what means this clamour! the shriek no succour wakes;
Were it not for the love of his people, offer what bid he may,
Max will remain here sitting till the final judgment day.

What the ear had not discover'd the vision had descried,
From below they saw him swaying on the pathless mountain's side;
There's a sound to heaven ascending of orisons and bells,
While from church to church in pilgrimage the tide of manhood swells.

At the mountain's foot a multitude in various garb appears,
A priest in their midst to heaven the sacrament uprears;
Where the crowds in mingled colours in the distant valley shone,
Max saw the glance and glitter of the golden pyx alone.

"Farewell now, life! The parting falls heavily on me,
Thou beckonest, the Inscrutable! I humbly follow Thee.
I seem like a tree full of blossoms, when thy lightning strikes its root,
It had later borne, how joyously! its wealth of golden fruit!

"Like the builder who a minster would to Thy glory raise,
And is not spared to finish the sanctuary of praise!
Like the priest on the steps of the altar who suddenly falls dead,
Before the invocation for his people's weal is said!

"Adieu! the aspirations that now my bosom fill,
And break, thou heart impulsive, that love and pleasure thrill;
Wither this hand—fame's guerdon will never shine for me,
For only God's best angel can my preserver be!"

In earnest supplication he sinks upon his knee,
Raises his eyes, invoking Heaven's succour fervently;
A hand is laid on his shoulder, he starts with a thrill of fear,
"Come home, thou art in safety!" rings cheerily in his ear.

And he sees a brawny mountaineer before him laughing stand,
Who grasps him, and points onward with a gesture of command;
With rope and steel and ladder soon a venturous path is ready,
If Max's footsteps stagger, his guardian's hand is steady.

He mounts Max on his shoulders where the dizzy chasms frown,
On a fairer throne and firmer Max never sat him down;
To the valley thus descending, his course all Tyrol cheers,
Though he rides in a strange fashion, at Max no scoffer jeers.

There is an old tradition, of many ages since,
That a messenger from Heaven wrought the rescue of the prince;
Yes, indeed, it was an angel, a spirit from above,
The love of faithful Tyrol, a loyal People's love.

From the precipice down-looking on the vale, a crucifix
Marks the spot whence Austria's scion saw the shining of the pyx;
Still lives the ancient legend, and in song will never cease
To stir a quicker heart-beat in every Tyrolese!

Max before Vienna.[21]

(August, 1490.)

I. THE REUNION.

N a hill-side, near Vienna, has stood, from days of yore
With delicate tracery chisell'd, a column tall and hoar;
Since the old days the Spinner at the Cross they've call'd the column,
And the old days rustle round it still, in legends quaint and solemn.

And thou, oh, gazing wanderer, who stand'st there now-a-days,
Thrill'st with the magic beauties the scenery displays;
And as the golden eagle with rustling plumage flies,
Sinks down upon thy heart inspiration from the skies.

There, with unrivalled grandeur, in matchless beauty bright,
The old imperial city breaks on the startled sight;
Around green woods and mountains, streams, meadows, and crops
like gold,
God's scroll of benedictions before thee lies unroll'd.

Round about this sea of stones, through the sloping valley lie,
Low in the broad savannas, and on the upland high,
Chapels, cottages, and castles, strewn on their ground of green,
Like white lambs by the side of the greater cattle seen.

And a stirring joyful murmur, the hollow rumble of drays,
And bells from a hundred steeples, shouts of joy and songs of praise;
In a thousand-fold echo swelling, it reaches the listener's ear,
As if it were hymning in chorus—"a happy folk lives here."

The earth with a gentle tremor quivers under thy feet,
The pulses of joy and life there so vigorously beat;
The breezes in light vibration ripple about thine ear,
And speak to thy heart in a whisper—"a happy folk lives here."

Not such to Max the aspect, when here he took his stand,
And gazed, with moistened vision, on the city and the land;
With him a powerful army of horse and foot appear,
Wide beaming helm and armour, and banner, shield, and spear.

Again he sees the towers of the vast cathedral gleam,
And there, beyond colossal piles, the Danube's azure stream,
That seems the faithful city with a girdle to enfold,
As the snake of a magician lies in watch before his gold.

The grey ancestral castle, afar he sees once more,
And well it might remind him of the better days of yore;
For once the Hapsburg banner serenely floated where
The hostile flag of Hungary, wild blowing, flouts the air.

And around stand, waste and empty, wide fields where once there roll'd
The yellow sheaves of harvest, like a waving sea of gold;
Did the reaper watch his season to cut the ripen'd grain,
Or did the Hungarian pasture his horse upon the plain?

See hill-top green on hill-top the azure stream along,
Once grapes hung there in clusters, once music swelled and song;
When the vine-dresser plucks thy clusters, he takes his own by stealth,
At night alone he rifles his vineyard's purple wealth.

Stand churches white and shining on all the hills around,
Where bell and song are silenced, stifled wailings only sound;

Thanks, thanks alone, once blended there with the merry chime of
bells,—
There is little left to pray for where Thrift with Freedom dwells.

Now sorrows rise on sorrows, and smoking cloud on cloud,
"Approach, and save thy people!" they seem to cry aloud;
And flaming sounds the answer return'd from Max's breast,
"Deliverance shall give thee prosperity and rest!

"My Austria, peerless Austria! all lands to thee must yield,
Truth shines as thy escutcheon, hold fast the diamond shield!
Rolls o'er thy head an atmosphere that blessing ever fills,
And silver are thy highways, and golden are thy hills.

"My greetings to thee, Austria! Yet how we meet again,
When misery shrouds thy hill-top, and misery sweeps thy plain--
Thine air the smoke of villages, thy rivers streams of blood,
Despair thine only chorus, and Truth thine only good!

"Thou city of my fathers! what a sad meeting ours!
See blood-soak'd banners flapping from my ancestral towers;
And I, alas! who gladly the crown of peace would bring,
Must crackling garlands of fire about thy turrets swing.

" Thou hast suffer'd, and must suffer, and yet thou wilt not fall,
The prison of suffering arches itself to a dome of joy for all ;
O, that a fitting guerdon might crown thy strength and truth,
And shine on thee from the darkness a day of spring and youth !"

II. THE SIEGE OF THE IMPERIAL PALACE.

THERE where the Kaiser's palace in ancient splendour lay,
Was encamp'd King Max's army, in magnificent array ;
For there his last resistance the Magyar planned undaunted,
And in the vaulted windows his grim artillery planted.

There princes once and courtiers dispensed their smiles of grace,
And he whom they vouchsafed one went home with joyous face ;
And he to whom from the window a look of love was sent,
Carried a beating heart with him—no matter where he went.

Where are you, imperial eagles ? What has frighten'd you away ?
Perch'd on St. Stephen's tower one ventures still to stay :

If he had not been made of marble, he, too, would have taken his
flight,
Or saw he the smiling morrow, after the stormy night?

Hark, the clangour of drums and trumpets! How it howls and
rages and cracks!
"Hic, up and in, my brothers!" How thunders the voice of Max!
The palace-walls with the battle-cries and the shower of bullets
quake;
If an emperor there were sleeping he would now be sure to awake.

The boldest of the warriors essay an escalade;
Are you climbing up the window of a pretty little maid?
Your sweetheart waits already, and from roses purple-red
She weaves a ruby coronet, to decorate your head.

By Max's side contending, a cavalier thus speaks;
"My prince, why comes so suddenly that pallor to thy cheeks?"
"Hush, friend, and were I pallid how otherwise could it be?
'Tis only the reflection of my armour that you see."

"Storm! up and in, my brothers!" Dust veils in clouds the walls,
From swords and throats of fire a shine of red flame falls;
A herdsman in the distance drives home his flocks to fold,
"A storm comes from Vienna—the lightning there behold!"

A cavalier by Max's side looked on the prince, and said,
"My prince, is it not blood there where your shoulder is so red?"
"Your sight's at fault, good fellow, the red you need not mind,
'Tis my mantle's purple lining turned outward by the wind."

"Ho! Bravo brothers, forward!" Now from the trembling walls,
Like flakes of blossoms in spring-time, a shower of bullets falls;
Almighty Heaven! loud cracking a smoking bastion crumbles,
And there a lofty parapet with a crash of thunder tumbles.

Up! up! over rubble and ruins, through the deadly breach they fly,
Now merrily thrills the drum-beat, and hark to the victor's cry!
Peace! peace! the colours of Hungary are draggled in the moats,
And from the ancestral castle the flag of Hapsburg floats.

As they rush in, the victors in the spacious halls behold
The corpses of Magyar warriors in heaps together roll'd;
And over them as sentinels, drawn scimitars in hand,
Like monumental seraphim the living Magyars stand.

Max greets their leader courteously, and gently takes his hand,
"Withdraw, ye noble champions, in peace to your own land;
Though enemies, I honour you. You've fought a manly fight;
I would we were contending for one land and one right!"

He spake; a fever seized him, and blood burst from his wound,
And with a pallid visage he sank upon the ground;
On a bier borne to a chamber, where no sound the stillness broke,
Soon from a heavy slumber, thanks to the Lord! he woke.

By his bed-side Convalescence the beautiful matron stood,
Kiss'd him on cheek and forehead, and staunch'd the flowing blood;
Without, a harp once sounded in the evening twilight dim,
And thus the winds of the Occident wafted the song to him:—

"From many an arrow, woman the heart of the loved one shields,
And but when the storm is over to the flood of suffering yields;
So the hero beckons his army where danger and glory be,
Before they bandage his wounds with the banners of victory.

"So both the tree resemble, which, from the hail and storm,
Protects, in its thick-leaved shadow, the tired wanderer's form;
But when the storm is over and the skies again are blue,
It shakes from its leaves and branches its own round drops of dew."

German Usage.[22]

(1495.)

N the grave sank Emperor Frederick; God rest him where he lies!
Max grasp'd the golden sceptre; to the sun may the eagle rise!
At Worms he held a Diet. Up, Princes, and hie thereto,
It is yours to promote and counsel, that light and right may grow.

Once in the musty council-hall Max rose, half-tired to death,
The dust of the parchments had nearly taken away his breath;
The prosy, long-headed speakers quite crazed him with form and fuss,
And he cried to his fool, " Friend Conrad, this is no place for us!"

He loves the faithful Conrad all other men above,
As a gardener in his garden watches every tree with love,
But selects one for himself, 'neath its foliage to repose,
When on day's sultry labours the shades of evening close.

They saunter'd through the streets, here and there, and up and down,
When they stopp'd before a mansion, of the stateliest in town;
Then Conrad spake: "My sovereign, shut your eyes without delay,
Many a man has read his eyes out on this spot before to-day.

"It is French, and by experience you know of a Frenchman's freaks,
Who does not read as he writes, and does not write as he speaks,
Who does not speak as he thinks, and does not compose as he sings,
So great in all things little, and so little in all great things."

A knight of France inhabited this house in princely state,
His escutcheon, brightly shining, hung high without the gate;
And on this gay escutcheon, upon a bright gold ground,
Inscribed in flourishing letters, these words were writ around:—

"May God bless him who reads it! My German bold, come out,
Here hang up thine escutcheon, if thou'rt ready for a bout;
And if, after knightly fashion and the laws of chivalry,
Thou conquerest, thereafter thy willing thrall I'll be."

The king pass'd on in silence, but soon on the knight's shield
A 'scutcheon hung, with the colours of Hapsburg on its field;
And with the dawn, awaiting, on an area of sand,
Opposed the king and the Frenchman in mortal combat stand.

How he swung his sword should I sing you, his good sword broad and true,
And how his spear he handled, I should sing you nothing new;
Should I say how without cessation he follow'd up stab with blow,
How the German deals with the Frenchman you've reason already to know.

Now higher the sun has mounted. The Frenchman lies on the sand,
The sword of victory shining is raised in Max's hand;
Like the conqueror St. Michael, with his falchion flaming bright,
He cries as he stands transfigured, "Thus strikes a German knight!

"To serve for life as my thrall is your voluntary doom,
And the rights my office gives me I shall instantly assume."
Three times he swung his sword round, "Rise up, my worthy knight;
Thus strikes a King and a German. Be brave as your sword is bright."

To all the land, ye singers, sing the prince's deed and word ;
To the jewel of your circle, lower, every knight, your sword ;
Crown the temples of the victor, fair women of Germany,
And shout to his glory, ye Germans, wherever Germans be.

Swell myriad juicy clusters round about Worms on the Rhine,
" Milk of our Lady," they call it, this luscious amber wine ;
Imbibe this milk, old man, it will make you again a child,
O Lord, give our land in thy bounty much milk so sweet and mild.

It flow'd from golden vessels on Max's board that night,
As if out of golden udders, so fresh and clear and bright ;
By Max's side how copiously the happy French knight tipples !
Down Conrad's throat how warmingly the genial liquor ripples !

The Frenchman raised the goblet, with ardour flamed his blood,
" Hail, Max, to thee, noble German, so gallant and so good !"
" Ho, ho !" cried Conrad, half fiercely, " now make a wager with me,
Which of us two to this toast can drink the most heartily."

How he swung his cup should I tell you, his cup the deep and true,
How he nimbly unsealed the bottles, I should tell you nothing new ;
How glass after glass he emptied, should I deem it worth while to tell,
That the German sticks close to the bottle, you certainly know full well.

Like shields flash their brimmers together, with a ring and a
rattle of might,
Their looks each other encounter like lances in the fight!
Who stood, who fell in the drinking?—it never came to light:
For neither could tell in the morning what happen'd over night.

Knights and Freemen.[23]

(1499.)

I. SWITZERLAND.

THIS rush into Switzerland, princes! what may its
meaning be?
Would you for once in your life-time look on a land
that is free?
Would you exchange the sceptre for a simple shepherd's stave,
Or in the soil of Freedom would you haply find a grave?

From a lofty Alpine summit look down upon this land,
It lies there like a volume all written by God's hand,
The mountains are the letters, as leaves the fields unroll,
Saint Gothard is only an asterisk in this gigantic scroll.

Know you what there is written? Oh, see it beams so bright,
Freedom stands there, ye princes! can ye read the page aright?
No chancellor engross'd it, it is no parchment chart,
And the red that burns in the signet is the blood of a people's heart.

Behold the mighty mountain—the Monk in the country hight,—
Around his brow the eagle sweeps in its heavenward flight;
His cowl is of rock, and the snow-crown becomes his temples well,
His prayer-book the starry heavens, the universe his cell.

When a Monk appears, there surely can be no lack of preaching,
In the thunder of the avalanche, in the cataract he is teaching;
Freedom! that is his text-word; good sirs, you do not smile,
It is clear the Monk is a heretic—he must go into durance vile.

Lo, in white veil the Maiden raises her modest head,
As Morning, the bridegroom, garlands her brow with roses red;
With various flowers embroider'd her green apparel gleams,
Where, like silver tissues inwoven, sparkle the crested streams.

Over her, arch'd to a cupola, behold the blue air streams,
The row of pointed glaciers a cathedral organ seems;
With a maid and an organ together, one cannot well be wrong
In listening with all assurance for music and for song.

Hear how her song magnificent thrills in the beating heart,
Freedom! Freedom! she sings so that all our pulses start:
By heavens! with such a harmony never sang daughters of earth,
And they who join in the chorus are surely of heavenly birth.

My Lords, will it not suit you? Is there no sound you will hear
Save a eunuch sing, or a sabre whistle it in your ear?
But this gigantic volume in Switzerland they read,
And hear the song of the Maiden, and the Preacher's sermon heed.

In Switzerland outbubbling freely the fountains spring,
Free sweep the clouds, and freely the birds in chorus sing;
From the glacier freely the chamois looks down on the thunder-storm,
And freely the west-wind bloweth o'er the freeman's lifeless form.

On the lofty Alpine summits the Swiss by thousands stand,
They look down on their country, and, clasping hand in hand,
They swear in death and in life ever firm and true to be,
And swear in death and in life to stand ever strong and free.

II. TWO HEROES.

STANDS graved at Kingsfield convent, on a monumental slab,
Here good King Albert perish'd, pierced by the assassin's stab:"
In the note books of astrologers, we see it often stand,
" This year a bloody comet was threatening the land."

At Kingsfield, in the Convent, on a stone the words appear:
" In the hope of resurrection Duke Leopold lieth here."
Thus a pillar to his grand-child a grey-hair'd peasant shows,
" Here once, now dust and ashes, a splendid temple rose."

In prayer King Max is kneeling Duke Leopold's grave beside;
Through Switzerland in vengeance as a Hapsburg he must ride:
As a monarch, to free Switzerland, bring slavery and chains:
As a man, the pulse of freedom beats wildly in his veins.

" Like a hero, noble ancestor, thou yieldedst up thy breath,
Throned on a pile of corpses, on Sempach's field of death;
Would I might perish in battle—as thou—so brave! so good!
But never will I crimson my sword with Freedom's blood."

He speaks and beckons: instantly, a knight strides from the crowd,
His arm as strong as an anvil, his mouth as stern as a shroud;
But that this arm can embrace one, and that this mouth can kiss,
Is told at home (in confidence) by many a laughing miss.

In peace, his eyes will moisten at a flower untimely blighted,
He relishes no goblet save when by his love invited;
But in war, skulls bleach'd and hollow he would fill with wine blood-red,
And quaff to the health of his lady, while he sat on heaps of the dead.

In a scroll the legend of knighthood is writ on his glancing shield,
Approved by his knightly bearing, and his valour in the field:
" My life belongs to my monarch, my soul to its source divine,
My heart is given to woman, and honour alone is mine."[24]

The prince bestows the truncheon of the general on the knight:
" Lead in my stead, my Furstenberg, our forces in the fight:
May Heaven guide you in mercy, and temper your weapon's glare;
Your vice-ensign be Victory, and Honour your standard bear!"

" Methinks, my friend, you fancy for fame there's little show,
Where a cow-horn is the clarion, and peasants are the foe:
But these hinds bring crown and purple to the test of the battle-
ground,
And many a proud heart quivers to hear that cow-horn sound."

On Uri's valley resteth the full moon's peaceful ray,
Once more the sun in parting looks back upon the day;
And long Saint Gothard's summit glows in the valley's night,
A giant altar blazing with a sacrificial light.

Where the swift Reuss foams and dashes through Uri's rocky glen,
Bearing aloft a banner, behold a crowd of men;
A Black Ox on a field of gold—lo, Uri's arms appear!
No yoke has ever press'd the neck of that unbroken steer.

There's a wooden house in the valley, on a little plot of green,
Where carved about the cornice in a rude scroll is seen,—
" I'm a free-born son of Switzerland and Harry Wohlleb hight,
This little house and its tenant stand only in God's might."

Before the threshold sits a man of venerable years,
Like a stripp'd field in autumn his hoary head appears;
A blooming little daughter sits smiling by his side,
As a rosebud decks a ruin with its beauty and its pride.

The earnest crowd approaching, the leader steps before,
And proffers the patriot standard to the veteran at the door:
" Friend Wohlleb, take this standard, with a heart as firm and bold,
As the mayor Nick Gutt at Sempach his banner bore of old."

The old man takes the banner, and lifts his reverend brow;
His guiding arm now trembles when he walks behind the plough;
But with a grasp unfaltering he holds that strong shaft high,
And hot words in wingéd cadence from his lips like eagles fly.

" Oh, keep, good Lord, thy people and thy servant in thy sight,
Who boldly raise their weapons for freedom and the right;
If thou will'st it, then, as firmly as a tower upon a rock,
This arm shall bear the standard through the battle's stormy
shock.

" Thou will'st we pay no homage to the purple—on our knee:
He bends no limb to mortal, who devoutly bends to thee;
Where with hostile foot the stranger our fathers' graves profanes,
Shall the knights' horses pasture—to trample their remains?

"Shall our children, pinch'd with hunger, with Death dispute the day,
And from knights' dogs snatch the morsels their masters throw away?
Shall their boys insult our greybeards? Shall we ever live to see
Their white hairs trampled in the dust? Oh God, that shall not be!

"Out now, out of thy scabbard! be true to me, my brand,
True as the good scythe proves itself in the skilful reaper's hand;
Twice only thine appointed days of labour thou hast mown,
Yet as Morat and as Grandson the well-reap'd fields are known!

"Holy banner, float for ever round the forehead of the free!
And from our flashing glaciers wave in sign of Victory!
Oh, awake in our valleys,—Freedom, heavenly maid, arise,
Thou hast made thy couch already where the Alps blend with the
skies."

So speaks the white-hair'd Wohlleb. His heart feels youthful now,
And the flutter of the banner cools the fever of his brow;
Thereon how sweetly bloweth the gentle evening air!
Or does Tell's shade approving lay his hand in blessing there?

Hear the Reuss as it foams and sparkles, and down through the
valley sings,
And from rock to rock impetuous like the chamois hunter springs;
See the full moon thereover glows out with blood-red fires,
And serenely on Saint Gothard the altar flame expires.

III. TWO DAYS.

ON the field in front of Frastenz, drawn up in battle array,
Stretched spear on spear in a crescent, the German army lay;
Behind a wall of bucklers stood bosoms steel'd with pride,
And a stiff wood of lances that all assaults defied.

Oh, why, ye men of Switzerland, from your Alpine summits sally,
And arm'd with clubs and axes descend into the valley?
"The wood just grown at Frastenz with our axes we would fell,
To build homesteads from its branches where Liberty may dwell."

The Swiss on the German lances rush with impetuous shock;
It is spear on spear in all quarters—they are dash'd like waves from a rock.
His teeth then gnash'd the Switzer, and the mocking German cried,
"See how the snout of the greyhound is pierced by the hedgehog's hide!"

Like a song of resurrection, then sounded from the ranks:
"Illustrious shade,[25] Von Winkelried! to thee I render thanks:

Thou beckonest, I obey thee! Up, Swiss, and follow me!"
Thus the voice of Henry Wohlleb from the ranks rang loud and free.

From its shaft he tore the banner, and twined it round his breast,
And hot with the lust of death on the serried lances press'd;
His red eyes from their sockets like flaming torches glare,
And in front, in place of the banner, wave the locks of his snow-white hair!

The spears of six knights together—in his hand he seizes all—
And thereon thrusts his bosom—there's a breach in the lances' wall.
With vengeance fired, the Switzers storm the battle's perilous ridge,
And the corpse of Henry Wohlleb to their vengeance is the bridge.

Then crackle the blows of the Switzers, as the hail falls on the fields,
Like sparks from the blacksmith's furnace, the sparks fly from the shields;
The blows of swords on the bucklers resound with a clash and clang,
As if in felling a forest a thousand axes rang.

When the woodman hews in the forest, the seedling he well may
spare,
That in time it may grow and flourish, and its mantle of foliage
bear;
Not thus in the forest of lances the Swiss their axes swung,
They spared neither stem nor scion—'twas alike with the old and
the young.

Knöring, the grey old oak-tree, sinks here with a mortal blow,
Ilsing, the cedar, beautiful, and rich in hope, lies low;
Wohlleb in death shouts "Victory!" and his followers join the cry,
In the plain that but now was a forest, where in blood two
armies lie.

The broad plain lay incarnadined, in bloody tapestry drest,
As the purple funeral trappings on a royal coffin rest,
There—instead of faded flowers—the knights' pale faces lay,
And Wohlleb like a lily, with his locks of silver grey.

And now like priests at the altar, with lifted eyes and hands,
By this great bier the army of enfranchised victors stands;
And their hands from carnage cleansing in the Illstrom's rushing
water,
They bury both friend and foeman with tears on the field of
slaughter.

You remember Castle Dorneck—and the castle's joyous throng,
At its gate the giant linden, in whose shade were dance and song :
See now its empty chambers—no arm the goblet swings,
Behold the quiet linden—there now no minstrel sings.

With broadswords, and with halberds, like stalks in a sea of wheat,
Below there in the valley the forces of Furstenberg meet ;
And the Swiss meet above on the mountain, where the scythes and
sickles glance,
Shouting for joy and singing like the reapers in harvest dance.

With a sneer now to his squires the German commander said,
"Take hence, to the reapers above there, this loaf of morning bread!"
You may spare the trouble of sending, proud knight, you may rue
your pride,
The Swiss will fetch it himself, perhaps, and leave you his thanks
beside.

See, he does not allow you to wait long—with shining ore he pays,
And the thanks he brings you'll be sure to remember all your days,
Though rough indeed is the coinage of the money that he brings,
Yet, mark, how bright it glistens—and hear how true it rings!

Ha, sword! thou art the money that we for tyrants wield,
The changers a free people, pay-day the battle-field;
Your money to-day, ye Switzers, ye've spared neither early nor late,
And many a German bearer has stagger'd under its weight.

Who is it, whose escutcheon in the hottest battle shines,
And who roars as roars the whirlwind among the groaning pines?
It can be only a freeman who so bravely fights—Ah, no!
It is Furstenberg—of his army the first in the foremost row.

In a fluttering black mantle, and bearing a cross of white,
Like a walking pall, a Switzer now storms into the fight:
The dean of Zug is the comer—to the Lord be the glory and thanks—
Welcome, your reverence, welcome, now to the patriot ranks!

To swing the brush full of water formerly was his wont,
That sprinkled the heads of the faithful from the minster's holy font;

Mark how he swings the sword now—how from it the red blood runs!
This is the brush and the water of Freedom baptizing her sons.

There stands a blood-stain'd warrior, on masses of the dead,
As the oak stands on the ridges, with the morning sunshine red;
It is only a Swiss who fights so! But he is not a Swiss,—
It is Furstenberg the German—what man fights better than this!

Hark, the horn of the herdsmen of Zug, with its shrill and horrible clang!
Storm! storm! in accents the wildest from the Unterwald boatmen rang!
Ho, ho, ye archers of Uri, the aim of your arrows is good!
Ho, ye vine-dressers of Soleure, your clusters already yield blood.

Borne high above all the others, what banner flutters there?
On a field of red and purple, lo! a grim and swarthy bear!
Yes, honest Berne, for thy banner the choice was wise and good;
The black bear, grim and angry, that welters deep in blood.

Lies one with a cloven brow there, who has fought in his last affray,
And smiles even in death o'er the lips of the hero play:

Only the free smiles dying—a Swiss is it? Ah, no!
It is again the Furstenberg, who in pain and death smiles so!

"Ye dextrous reapers of Switzerland, your sickles cut to the blood,
Ye lusty threshers of Switzerland, your threshing is strong and good:"
In the midst of his army's corpses thus he groan'd with his latest breath,
Still true to his knightly legend, as in life so also in death.

Like gather'd sheaves of the harvest, the knights around lie dead,
And in the midst their leader, like a poppy purple-red;
On the stripped and desert corn-field the sun's red beams are cast,
Where the reapers devour in silence their eventide repast.

See there the fearful charnel-house, where Freedom garners her grain;
There, heap'd like ears of the harvest, the bleaching bones remain;
When, sometime, the first morning of the eternal spring draws near,
In its fulness then, oh Freedom, thy harvest shall appear!

Oh, Dorneck, beautiful Dorneck, how dear thou art to me!
How gladly does the minstrel return again to thee!
Thou blessèd pair, that lingerest in the shade of the linden tree,
Long may'st thou look thus blessèd, on a beautiful land and free!

IV. TWO CORPSES.

IN Switzerland lie the corpses of two devoted men,
The one in the field at Frastenz, the other in Dorneck's glen;
Both, in the shock of battle, drew in pain their latest breath,
They nothing had in common—but nobleness and death.

Like a strong tower of rock was of one the lofty form,
Which after a long defiance has yielded to the storm;
His heart a spent volcano, now feelingless and sear,
With showers of flame once menaced death to him who ventured near.

The other an ancient altar, now crumbled for many a year,
Whereon the flame of sacrifice had once burn'd bright and clear;
His heart the sun's mild image, where the hues of the rainbow met,
But now the rainbow is faded, the sun in clouds is set.

One's eyes were closed by a woman, with tears and sobbings wild,
This woman, is it not Freedom? It is the old man's child.
In the hearts of a grateful people his eulogy is read,
And his free native country is the monument of the dead.

But the other unlamented, deserted, and alone,
Is there none to close his eyelids? Does none his fate bemoan?
Remains there nothing true to him? His faithful battle-horse
Scares away the impatient ravens that gather round his corse.

The one was proud as a monarch, and yet he was only a hind;
Freer than monarch the other, yet just and of simple mind:
The Swiss says—"There lies Wohlleb"—pride mantling in his cheeks,
"And here the Furstenberger"—with a shudder as he speaks.

A little chest, where Freedom might her bridal favours store,
The coffin of one resembles—whose lid this legend bore;
"I'm a free-born son of Switzerland, and Harry Wohlleb hight,
This little house, and its tenant, stand only in God's might."

Bedeck'd with blood-bought jewels, for a prince's coffer fit,
Was the coffin of the other, on which these words were writ:—
"My life belong'd to my monarch, my soul to its source divine,
My heart was given to woman, and honour alone was mine."

Oh, Honour, Princes, Woman! Is this your guerdon, indeed?
Is thy scorn spat on the tombstone, oh, world, thine only meed?
Ye twain sleep softly—but tell me, ye who yet watch and weep,
As Wohlleb or as Furstenberg, would you sleep the eternal sleep?

V. FREEDOM.

WHO is it that to Max now may bring the fatal story,
Of the slaughter of his army, on this day so dark and gory?
It is the wise Pirkheimer, who fought a noble fight,
With pen and sword alike, for the cause of truth and right.

How did the prince receive it? Was he overwhelm'd with woe?
In tears did he deplore it? Despair, indeed? Ah! no!
The owl shrieks when the archer through her breast the arrow wings;
The royal swan, though wounded to the death, groans not, but—sings.

The king embark'd at Kostnitz, in the dead hour of night,
Before him the lake so quiet, above him the stars so bright!
The moon in his eye look'd softly, as if she spake from her heart,
"In my day, methinks, I have noticed full many a sharper smart."

The waves, too, seem'd to whisper as they play'd about his prow:
"We have borne on our bosom many a one more to be pitied than thou;"
And the winds, with a coaxing flattery, wafted into his ear—
"We have oftentimes before this dried many a bitter tear."

And as the prince in the morning on shore at Lindau went,
The rosy dawn caressingly over his pale cheeks bent,
As if from her azure canopy of air she stoop'd to say—
" Many pale cheeks I have redden'd, cheeks paler than thine to-day."

Clear as the empyrean, as the moonshine pure and light,
Like the lake's unruffled surface, Max's soul is calm and bright;
The mists from his heart are lifted, for home and peace are found;
He bows his head to the strand—he kisses the German ground.

The mountains of Switzerland gorgeously glisten before the prince;
Thus many a monarch and minstrel have seen them before and since;
Hail to the noble monarch, to his happy people hail!
When he looks in the face of Freedom with an eye that does not quail.

But where may now the Victors, the patriot Switzers, be?
Where, now, is the camp of the heroes? what their meed of victory?
Where sounds the song that burneth with freedom's deathless flame?
Where do these brave men build themselves their monument of fame?

See there the milking cow-herd, the fisher here in his skiff,
The ploughman and the reaper, the hunter upon the cliff;
You see the heroes already—to seek them there is no need,
Around a free air and free country—these are the victor's meed.

Hark! the goblet clinks at the table, in the wood the rifle cracks,
Twangs the horn of the Alpine shepherd, ring the blows of the woodman's axe;
Here the tinkle from Alpine herds, there the peal of the vesper bells;
This is the song of Freedom! How grandly its music swells!

Truth, courage, love, sincerity, faith, loyalty and right,
These are the holy seven in the blended ray of light!
The colour of that rainbow, whose flaming arch is bent,
High over the Swiss mountains, as Freedom's Monument!

The Fight at the Grave.[26]

(1503—1505.)

I. THE TREASURE AT BURGHAUSEN.

THE Duke George of Bavaria lay on the bier of the dead,
No coronet gleam'd in mockery upon his hoary head;
No son invoking blessings look'd in the sick man's eye,
In death to close his eyelids no loving wife was by.

To whom now shall the vassals renew their oath of fealty?
Who shall enjoy at Burghausen the chattels and the realty?
Hark, the rattle of shield and broadsword! is that the funeral song?
See hosts in mailèd armour! is it thus the mourners throng?

First, Albert of Bavaria seized the Prince's coronet,
Such was the will of the dead man! on whom would it better set?
And Robert, the youthful Palsgrave, Burghausen storms with the cry,
"If I only clutch the fur first, I'll manage the hat by and bye!"

Approached King Max's herald, who aloud to the fighters said,
" At once lay down your weapons, break not the peace of the dead ;
I have not given laws to the empire that they should be made a
game,
So I summon you both to the throne to present a peaceful claim."

Now Albert lays his coronet before the feet of the King,
" Before your throne, my sovereign and judge, my rights I bring :"
But Robert of Burghausen laughs in his sleeve the while,
" You minniken King, these antics but serve to make me smile."

In the treasury at Burghausen stand many chests of gold,
Which precious metals and brilliants and gems and jewels hold ;
And, fashion'd of pure silver, around like sentries stand,
In twelve colossal statues, the apostolic band.

" Welcome, good sirs," said Robert, " I honour your condition,
Yet it seems to me, right slackly you execute your mission ;
The Lord said to you, 'Go out now and spread abroad My word,'
But for years outside this palace I'm sure you have never stirr'd."

" True to your master's calling, I now will send you forth
On a pilgrimage and preachment to the south, and to the north."

So doom'd to a second martyrdom in the furnace's roar and flash,
He melted the twelve apostles, and coin'd them into cash.

Then abroad in all directions the silver pieces glisten'd,
How powerful was their preaching! how gladly the people listen'd!
And no sooner very gently had they knock'd at Kuffstein's gate,
Than Pinzenauer open'd it—too civil to let them wait.

The golden keys of the fortress he sends to Sir Robert duly,
"Most potent prince, I find you a wonderful locksmith truly:"
Bohemia sent her strong men—Bohemia, land of strength,
"Your foes shall feel our daggers, and measure our lances' length."

Came the mountaineer of Hainault: My arm belongs to thee!
Came the chivalry of Luxembourg: And thine our banners be!
As they throng'd in the time of Peter to Zion's holy hill,
So from far and near the pilgrims the castle of Robert fill.

Arouse ye, Max and Albert! ye champions good and brave!
Now the warm fur is Robert's, the hat may be hard to save.
Ah, sturdy Count, it may be you are safe from Max to-day;
But a Captain—little looked for—now mingles in the fray!

Victor in every land, he remains still unsubdued,
His castle is impregnable, though a little house of wood!
He looks on thee, thou art pallid, and he kisses away thy breath,
And the Captain who assails thee, the name of the Captain is Death.

Who is it by Robert's coffin, the man with snow-white hair?
It would almost seem that Robert himself were kneeling there,
So grim he looks and defiant, with his powerful fist clench'd tight,
Only it seems as if sorrow had made him old in a night.

That is the Palsgrave's father. He rose and snatch'd the brand,
With a grasp quick and convulsive, from his dead son's icy hand;
"Thy pale cheek I cannot re-colour, but thy sword I will dye red,
Up, up! ye warriors, follow me, Sir Robert is not dead!"

II. THE BOHEMIAN FIGHT.

AS the sun sank slow and golden adown its western track,
It look'd on two encampments in the field of Mengesbach,
Two glaciers saw impending over a lovely vale,
Which shall thunder down an avalanche, in the sweep of the morrow's gale.

One of the camps as quiet as Carthusian convent lay,
Not a sound above a whisper was heard from that arm'd array;
Two men were passing silently from silent tent to tent,
The men seem'd Max and Albert, on earnest business bent.

But things went on right merrily in the camp on the other side,
There was singing, there was ringing, as if it were Carnival tide;
Here one his broadsword sharpen'd, there another snored by its side,
While a third sang to his charger—"Oh, would you were my bride!"

The Bohemian lounged by his beer and the Palatine sat by his wine,
The moon from the swarthy welkin peer'd out with a pallid shine;
"How it trembles, up above there, like a timid little maid,
A cowardly companion—of the show of blood afraid."

"Yes, blood is our business to-morrow"—the many tipplers roar;
"Three German cowards I'll do for"—"and I will gobble up four;"
"Drink good luck to Bohemia!" and they drink it with all their might,
Far and wide the clink of the goblets resounds through the sombre night.

And higher the moon ascending, slow on its eastern track,
Still looks on the two encampments in the field of Mengesbach;

Two brothers sees in the distance, who in sweet slumber rest,—
The dagger of one to-morrow shall pierce the other's breast.

"Ye Bohemian musicians, strike up the hop and the reel!"
Now with jovial steps the tipplers in dizzy circles wheel;
Hark! hark! to the drums and the trumpets! And a voice the crowd salutes,
"Why blend the blast of the trumpets with the music of the flutes?"

And hark again! A mortar in the field loud thundering rang,
And forth from his tent in a moment the old Count Palatine sprang;
"I know this voice full surely! 'Tis the nightingale of Max,
Its song to the full moon singing. How the music crashes and cracks!"

The mortars thunder louder, and the broadswords rattle and ring,
You may dance and we'll make the music—we'll pipe for you and sing;
While the cry of "Max and Albert" louder and deeper breaks,
And the camp from its hurly-burly like the trump of the judgment wakes.

Then from their tents they stagger'd, and for sword and shield ran wild,

St. Nepomuk to the rescue! St. Wenzel, be kind and mild!
Then one, in seeking his helmet, took a pot from the hearth instead,
And one broke his fiddle to pieces on the first best comer's head.

Yet bravely fought the Palsgrave—for two his good sword fell,
And the arm of the grey old hero the shade of the son guides well;
Now rallying around him the gallant warriors close,—
For where Bohemians battle there is never lack of blows.

Who lies there under his charger, in the very thick of the fray?
It is the King! God help him! for he needs God's help to-day:
Who hews—his guardian angel! a path to him with his sword?
In battle and victory famous—that is Eric, Brunswick's lord!

Hush'd is the roar of the mortars. Clouds of dust obscure the skies,
When the prince, again in safety, to the heavens lifts up his eyes:
Before him stand Eric and Albert,—their faces beam with delight,
With fervour both exclaiming,—"We conquer in the fight."

The hand of his preserver the King presses gently now,
"Seest thou the star of morning on the blue heaven's distant brow?
Like that star, a welcome messenger, I saw thee come to save.—
Henceforth on thy escutcheon its smiling image grave."

Higher mounts the star of morning in the Orient's flecker'd rack,
And it sees two camps no longer in the field of Mengesbach;
But it sees two glaciers crumbled on a desolated plain,
And sees two brothers lying there, by brothers' daggers slain.

III. MAX BEFORE KUFFSTEIN.

FROM Kuffstein's giant ramparts Pinzenauer turns his eye,
With scorn and proud defiance, where Max's legions lie;
As a vulture from his eyrie, with an eye that does not quail,
Sees a hunter aim his rifle in the deep and distant vale.

Serenely calm and confident, Max lifts a glance on high,
Where Kuffstein's rocky battlements stand out against the sky;
As the hunter from the valley looks up to the vulture's nest,
"The rifle well may carry where the foot has never prest."

From a hundred mortars upwards fly thundering ball on ball,
Powerless, trackless, from the parapets rebounding rattle all;

As the showers of early blossoms on burnish'd armour play,
Or as on the rocks of ocean is dash'd the crested spray.

There they saw the Pinzenauer on the ramparts take his stand,
With a stout bundle of switches that he carried in his hand;
Where the shot of the besieger struck, in scorn he downward bent,
And with his broom of switches swept the dingy battlement.

" Ay, ay, thou mocking raven, take care of thyself," cried Max,
" Look from thy bundle of switches there does not leap an axe;"
His eye the while flash'd lightning, for his spirit was sorely stirr'd,
Deeper wounds than the keenest stiletto the stab of a scornful word.

Now rattling over the fortress the pitch-smear'd garlands fly,
In vain,—for light and harmless on the unscathed walls they lie;
While the Pinzenauer leisurely thereby his viands drest;
" Patience," cried Max, " I'll presently send hunger as your guest."

Thus for three weeks together Max in his tent held rest,
Already hunger invites himself to his table as a guest:
Did not Max promise to send him as a guest to Kuffstein's door?
Whom man employs as a messenger, he must prove himself before.

Among the tents there's a clamour. What means this noisy tramp?
See herds and herdsmen crowding into the royal camp:
"Hans Pinzenauer sends greeting, and spares what spare he may,
So that for once your majesty may have a plenteous day."

Now, though in patience abounding, Max felt his patience fail,
You could hear the heart-throb sounding beneath his coat of mail;
"It is time," quoth he, "incontinently, this nest of traitors to
break up;"
So he sent to his Innsbruck arsenal for Purlepaus and Wake-up.[17]

The king who wielded the sceptre the match-cord seized instead,
And he wielded the one and the other with a master's hand and
head;
On the throne there was no monarch his equal in splendour and
might,
On the field of battle his equal in courage and strength no knight.

The walls of Kuffstein tremble where his death-dealing volleys
sweep,
His Wake-up instead of waking sends many a soul to sleep;
His Purlepaus into the bulwarks strikes with resounding din,
Huzza! the giant ramparts loud thundering tumble in.

Lo, shining in robes of satin, with their peaceful wands of green,
Issuing forth from the castle, two boys in white are seen,
As the first two blossoms budding in the genial breath of spring,—
But they meet a stern and menacing dismissal from the King.

The gates of the castle are open'd and issues thence again,
In procession slow and solemn, an earnest band of men;
A hero firm and gloomy, Hans Pinzenauer before,
His beard was long and swarthy, and black the garb he wore.

Ah! how on Max's forehead the clouds converging lie,
His face glows as the tempest that lurks in the evening sky:
Like the shine of the fiery lightning his blue eye flames and quivers,
Woe to the head of the doom'd one the forkèd lightning shivers!

The warriors tremble—never had they seen him in this vein,
With timid eyes and downcast in silence they remain;
In the solemn circle echoing resounds his fatal word,
As in the wood the echo of the thunderbolt is heard.

"Up! whet thine axe, thou headsman! Death be their guerdon meet,
This humble garb of repentance ill suits their scoffing conceit:

I'll brook no intercession—who to plead for them appears,
My fist a tingling answer shall write about his ears."

"My prince, I will not entreat thee to spare my worthless life,
Long have my treasures mouldered—my father, child, and wife:
My heart and garb betoken that for me no sun may shine,—
I beg for one thing only—a goblet full of wine."

So spake the Pinzenauer—his firm hand did not fail,
As the monarch he confronted his cheek did not grow pale;
Like a crucifix of bronze on a marble monument,
Such sadness and solemnity, with strength and firmness blent!

"My king, to thy good fortune! I pray thee, deeply think,
How full it is of meaning, when one on the next world's brink,
From his heart's depth sincerely can pray God save King Max!"
He spoke and without blenching bowed his head to the bloody axe.

Ten of his true companions follow his fatal path,
On the king's visage pity now takes the place of wrath:
To show his enemies mercy the king is nothing loth,
And silently he imprecates the hasty, wicked oath.

"Hold, hold, my prince," cried Eric of Brunswick, undismay'd,
"Though it may rouse your anger, the word must yet be said;

Away with your bloody sergeants, and wash from the axe its stains,
That is wet with the blood, and the best blood, that flows in human veins.

"For cowards and for scoundrels, not the bold and brave in fight,
Is the headsman's block made ready, and the headsman's axe made bright,
If for bravery and boldness this be the guerdon due,
His axe bid the headsman sharpen, first of all, my King, for you."

True to his oath, Max gave him a gentle blow on the ear,
Gave his hand a gentle pressure, to his breast then drew him near;
"Thanks, thanks, my noble Eric, the brave word comes from the heart,
Let the rest unharm'd and scathless from hence in peace depart."

The little church of Ainleffen, near Kuffstein, marks to-day,
The spot where by Max's bidding the bones of the victims lay;
And once when he came to Tyrol, thereafter,—in fervent prayer
Tradition tells that a peasant saw the king kneeling there.

When Max came home victorious with music and with song,
Appear'd an humble poet in the courtiers' golden throng;
And begged them to his majesty in a laurel wreath to take up
An elegant little poem on Purlepaus and Wake-up!

IV. THE PEACE BANQUET.

AT Cologne the Palsgrave cordially to Albert gave his hand,
And King Max as mediator drew close the friendly band;
Now each was well contented—with all that he could get,—
The Palsgrave took Burghausen—Albert the Coronet.

Max gave an evening banquet to the lords and their array,
For the monarch loved to mingle the serious and the gay;
As men the gloomy sepulchre with wreaths of roses twine,
And deck the solemn altar with the pendant lustre's shine.

There is dancing, there is masking, and jovial song resounds,
There are pastimes without number, there is revelling without bounds;
While the re-united princes, with jest and laughter loud,
And arm in arm enfolded, are sauntering through the crowd.

Then from the circle of maskers the princes stepp'd before
A form in the guise of Ganymede, who a brace of goblets bore;
One was a golden goblet, of metal pure and bright,
A hollow skull the other, smooth-rubb'd, and ghastly white.

"A glass at this hour may suit you, my masters, I opine,
One fluid fills both chalices—wine, clear and luscious wine;
But the frame-work is dissimilar—it is for you to choose,"—
Both princes seize the goblet and the hollow skull refuse.

"I'd have wager'd any money that you the skull had chosen,"
(Between ourselves) the speaker was Conrad von der Rosen;
"It was much more in your fashion,"—thus he ventures on his jeers,
And again in the crowd of maskers like a shadow disappears.

Thereupon, in the garb of a herald, to the princes a man drew nigh,
To recognize King Max in him required no curious eye;
The shoulders of both princes he deck'd with a scarf of price,
Whereon stood a double eagle inwoven with this device:

"Of heads, to the German Eagle, we do not give a pair,
That one head may bite the other, and the common plumage tear;
That it may see in the distance the dangers that arise,
For this the German Eagle has a double pair of eyes."

The Last Victory.[28]

(1513.)

I. THE LEAGUE OF THE PRINCES.

WO allied hosts are lying in the fields round Terouenne,
Hate of the French has rallied these camps of arméd men;
Here the serried might of England to the breeze its banner flings,
And Germany's double eagle unfolds its mighty wings.

The Rhine severs French and Germans. What steed, oh Germany,
With bold spring carried thereover the sword of vengeance and thee?
Hate was the high-mettled leaper, the charger of swarthy wing;
Love only, the bird with the olive, outflies his venturous spring.

A sea severs French and Britons. And who the sea has spann'd,
With a bridge, for the hosts of England to enter the Frenchman's
land?
Hate is the name of the builder, who bridges both stream and sound,
Love only builds more grandly—for his building, look around!

Before the camp of their people sauntereth a noble pair,
Harry the youthful Briton, and Max with snow-white hair;
And wide and smooth extended, like a lake before their eyes,
From Terouenne to Guinegate a field for battle lies.

By Harry's side strode Talbot, as in Heaven's tent appear
Red Mars the bloody planet and silver Hesperus near;
See Conrad von der Rosen by the side of his master follow,
As the placid star of morning attendeth on Apollo.

As Max looks round reflecting, what thoughts his spirit strike!
How in this world of ours are the new and the old alike!
Since I won here my first victory some thirty years have past,
It may be that to-morrow I here may win my last.

See there the castle's bulwarks, the belfry, tower and gate;
See here the plain extended,—the past is the present's mate;
The earth and the face of the heavens the self-same aspect wear,
Only wider is the grave-yard, and whiter is my hair.

And yet how changed! generation to generation succeeds,
Oft has the harvest been gather'd, oft has spring sown its seeds;
The air has storm'd and whisper'd, the sun has risen and set,
But through the plain remorseless stalks the old hatred yet.

Then interrupted Harry, " Look, you must not forget,
Love binds our arms together, a priceless amulet:
No time, however distant, this friendly league shall sever,"—
Max pressed him to his heart,—" It shall live, my friend, for ever!"

In silence serene and sober now stand the royal pair,
Deep, azure, clear and silent broods the eternal air;
The plains about are silent, so level and so wide,
Dumb echoes of Forever! they seem on every side.

When in the sombre cathedral the notes of the organ ring,
And sounds the solemn Sanctus, like the whisper'd breath of spring;
Some loud sneezer in the pauses the cathedral music mars,
What becomes then of the ecstasy that swept us to the stars?

So Conrad now winks and twitches, and writhes and wrinkles his brow,
He has something to disburthen, it must never out or now;
Jingling his caps and bells there, he cries right merrily,
" Let me hear how old, my princes, you imagine me to be."

" So old that for growing wiser in faith there's little scope,
And yet at this very moment you're old enough for the rope;"
Thus snarlingly and grimly the bitter Talbot spoke,
But with friendlier words and gentler, King Harry took the joke.

" His teeth mark the age of the courser, his antlers the age of the deer,
Man's age is mark'd on his visage in signs sufficiently clear;
Boy is writ on your forehead, and man is writ on your cheek,
Which am I to believe now? Where the truth lies, prithee speak!"

The emperor Max then laughing,—" If our proverb speak the truth,
With every seventh year ended, there's a change in man forsooth;
Now ever since I have known you a fool you've always been,
From which—seven years I reckon you never yet have seen."

" Ah, how you flatter! I number—more than two hundred year';
Of the leagues of Blois and Cambray I stand survivor here;
Each of these leagues was made for a century—you see—
But now you make me hope for a full—eternity."

II. GUINEGATE.

THERE stood the allied armies, drawn up in battle array,
And France's legions opposite on the field of Guinegate lay;
The weight of his shining helmet Max lifted from his head,
With quick step strode before them, and to his soldiers said:

"Ye warriors never conquer'd, do you recognize this face?
Its features through Time's bleaching and Time's furrows can you trace?
Ask of these well-known battle-fields if they remember it not!
Ask of the hosts before us,—by Heavens, they've scarce forgot!

"Yet never will this visage before their glances pale,
This eye meets theirs with a courage and a hate that never quail;
And when the crown of victory encircles this grey hair,
It becomes the head right royally, if the locks be grey or fair.

"Inscribe your names, my brothers, this day in the Book of Glory,
Your ink the blood of your enemy, let the sword record your story:

My sword! long-tried and faithful, this day remain the same,
Oft already as a plough-share thou hast plough'd the field of fame.

"And thou, my faithful war-horse, my comrade in the fight,
Full often hast thou borne me where victory's path was bright:
Thanks! thanks! once more the greybeard in his last battle bear,
To the goal of the bloody race-course! The Prize now beckons
there."

And as the German emperor his limbs in the saddle swung,
Shouts of "Hail, Maximilian!" from the hosts assembled rung;
A dark cloud at the moment o'er the face of the heavens past,
Which mask'd the azure welkin, and a baleful shadow cast.

"Ho, brothers! behold the heavens themselves come to our aid,
As they share between the combatants the equal light and shade;
Then up! the shade's refreshing in the hot hours of fight,
When the conqueror turns homeward, his path may again be
bright."

The trumpets bray, and the legions storm on exultingly,
The banners over them floating like sea-gulls over the sea;
The ranks close pressed together the mounted squadrons form,
And on with the infantry, shielded by a forest of halberds, storm.

Ah, how in battle the emperor struck about, never tired!
Like a dancer on Shrove Tuesday with the whirl and the music
fired;
How like the tongue of a tiger his sword lapped the crimson gore,
How proudly the long-maned charger his gallant master bore!

And forward, irresistible, forward storms the dense array,
The Frenchmen spur their horses and throw their weapons away;
Ye gallant sons of France, now, I pray you look to your skin,
Your sword sticks to its scabbard! Some rogue may have glued
it in.

Looking on from a hill in the distance, Sir Conrad stood at leisure:
"I should see for once in a life-time a fight with so much pleasure!
All the way up here I've clamber'd," (and here I'm afraid he
swears,)
"In the hope of seeing a battle,—but it's only a hunt of hares."

The roar of the mortars slacken'd, and hush'd was the weapons'
clang,
Instead of the cries of battle, the conqueror's clarion rang;
Clouds of dust the course envelop where the harried Frenchmen
run,
While the Germans shout exulting,—Hurrah, the victory's won!

That day the Germans and Britons in amity join'd hands,
And the haughty neck of the Frenchman trod in the bloody sands;
The Battle of the Spurs they call it even to the present day,
As instead of his sword the Frenchman put only his spurs in play.

His horse stagger'd dead in the saddle as Max leap'd from his back,
As he thrust it into the scabbard, he heard his old sword crack;
As if both spake like warning, This victory is your last!
And his heart too said, foreboding, Your day of victory's past!

Then smiling Max in sadness, "The faithful ploughshare breaks,
The plough-horse dies,—with feebleness the arm of the ploughman
shakes;
The bloody field of glory I have plough'd for the last time,
May my field be found not seedless in the spring of eternal prime!"

As home return the squadrons with songs of exultation,
Max leans his head on his bosom in silent contemplation;
Then breaks from out the weikin the sun's resplendent ray,
And victory's green garland still nods in his locks of grey.

III. THE PILGRIMAGE.

A STATELY castle rises not far from Terouenne,
Where Max sits at a banquet with a band of trusty men;
The Abbot of Dendermonde, the emperor's ancient friend,
And courtier, fool and warrior in the merry crowd attend.

From a pleasant hunting party just arrived, the jovial throng
Heard many a hunter's story, trill'd many a hunter's song;
The jolly jests of the hunter about the table flew,
And at game long since digested the spear was hurled anew.

Hark, hark! the notes of an anthem ascend from the vale below,
As pilgrims in procession are wont to sing as they go;
And a tinkling chime in the pauses to the castle softly swells,—
Max rose from his seat to listen to the peal of the pilgrims' bells.

" Fill your glasses, quick, to a bumper, for heaven's sake," Conrad cried,
And saluted his nearest neighbour with an elbow in his side;
" To drown this devil's psalmody at the top of your voices hollow,
For if Max gets wind of this bell now, be sure he is bound to follow."

With a sharp but crystal ringing the glasses together rattle,
" Long life to the noble victor in the bloody Guinegate battle!"
Max lifted a menacing finger to Conrad with a smile,
Bending his head with courtesy to his merry guests the while.

" In the victor you honour the victory, but forget not the praises belong
To Him who dispenses the victory; we are weak—but God is strong;
Hear the pilgrims who go to St. Alban's with music and solemn song,
I propose, my friends and brothers, that we join the pious throng."

Spake Conrad von der Rosen: " In sooth, I can hardly go;
As I from the hill-top yonder look'd down on the fight below,
I was kept so long a-standing that my right leg is almost broke,
And my eyes the clouds of powder have blinded with steam and smoke."

Then the equerry Emershoff grimly rose from his seat and cried,
" Permit me to saddle the horses, as we all will have to ride;
For if we go on foot here in our hunting boots and spurs,
We shall get finely entangled in the bushes, briars and furze."

Out of his right-hand pocket the Abbot a volume draws,
" This pilgrimage I advise against, list to the ancient saws;

One is, ‘ Post prandium pausa,’—rest awhile after you eat,
‘ Nec sta, nec mea sine causa,’—above all a nap is meet."

Then seriously the emperor: " Good sirs, your jesting spare,
Who ever heard of a patient that was made the worse by prayer?
Who enters a church on horseback? read me this riddle, I beg,
And, Conrad, this pious pilgrimage perchance may heal your leg."

Forth from the gates of the castle Max issues with reverend brow,
With a sourish mien and downcast the companions follow now;
Over the pilgrims unfolded the banners flutter and swing,
And on their way to St. Alban's the solemn anthems ring.

Many a handsome gold piece Max gave the priest that day,
When the pilgrims return'd from the chapel, where they had knelt
to pray;
The old man stammer'd his blessing, and his thanks—" By heaven,
I wis,
Since St. Alban's was St. Alban's, it never saw sight like this."

With lustrous shine in the heavens the constellations wheel,
When the pilgrims repair to the tavern for a spicy evening meal;
The dancers whirl in the mazes—down outside and up the middle,
To the sound of guitar and cymbal, to the sound of bagpipe and
fiddle.

What pretty maids there are, now! Hic, hic! and three times hic!
How the petticoats flirt and flutter! And the lads they are nothing
but eye!
In spite of his spurs then Emershoff, in the dust that he raises,
whirls,
And see how his arm encircles the slender waists of the girls!

In spite of his lame leg, Conrad kept very good time in the dance,
In spite of smoked eyes, he squinted at the girls with a merry
glance;
And a bumper toss'd off to the Abbot, "Come, father, another bout;"
But, muttering his saws in Latin, the old Abbot trundled out.

"It is well to rest at evening, Hem! hem! 'Post cœnam stabis,'
Or take an evening saunter, 'aut mille passus meabis'!"
Then from his left-hand pocket a rosary he drew,
And up and down he waddled in the moonlight and the dew.

Above, Max leaned reflecting, alone in a quiet nook,
Whence on the throng beneath him he cast a smiling look;
And thought in still home sickness of the past and of the far,
Where in youth's empyrean shone life's serenest star.

Max in Augsburg.

(1518.)

I. ENTRY.

HE heart of every mortal has an atlas of its own:
The places on Life's journey which joy and love have known,
A clear pure light in the heavens points out to him from afar,—
As over the Lord in the manger the wise men beheld the star.

" Oh, star that shin'st over Augsburg, how brightly thou point'st to the place,
Like truth in the eye of manhood, like kindness in woman's face,
Over the days that have vanish'd blending the light and the gloom,
And strewing with dulcet promises the days that are yet to come."

Thus Max to the trusty companions who rode with him that day,
Before them the lovely city in the midst of the Lechfeld lay;

But what do they see in the woods there that looks so like a camp?
Is it the King of the gipsies with his people on a tramp?

Thereon replied Sir Conrad: "If I can trust my eyes,
There, with his tribe of gipsies, King Amor's encampment lies:
But they seem not bent upon travel, its toils their little feet wound,
What wonder, for vagabond women are lying there on the ground.

"Indeed the camp is a marvel, where needles figure for lances,
Where for shields—on the trees suspended—mirror on mirror glances;
Many arrows lurk in the pupils of eyes brown, blue and black,
And as light and heavy artillery the large and little tongues clack.

"If the heart of every mortal has an atlas of its own,
Then on their maps as a comet this star of yours is shown;
Like the marshal's rod in anger its flame over Augsburg burns,
Reminding of bitter departures, and menacing sad returns."

"That we may share thy protection, homewards, good Lord, be pleased,"
Cried one of the women, who gently the emperor's bridle seized;
"Oh, carry thy daughters home again to the prudent magistrate,
To the sons carry their sisters, its children to the state."

Then the little lasses hung upon his stirrup and his rein,
Clung to the hem of his garment, to his horse's tail and mane;
The emperor permitted it, the while his thoughts might be,
"My purple may shelter you, forsooth, my grey hairs shelter me!"

Thus rode thence the procession. Sir Conrad rides in the rear,
And keeps up an audible thinking, that reaches his comrade's ear:
"Oh, Max, thou strangest of sportsmen! Lo, the manner of birds that sing,
In thy springes of pack-thread and horse-hair, sprawling and fluttering.

"Oh, Max, thou strangest of gardeners! Is't for a tilt of roses
That the tail and mane of your charger are deck'd with such piebald posies?
Oh, Max, thou strangest of emperors! What a splendid guise you wear!
What a scuffle among your pages the tail of your train to bear!"

At the gate stand the people and council. And they all think it vastly queer,
As the emperor and Amor's gipsies in this strange fashion appear;
But around them wave in protection his mantle's ample folds,
As all of us Love all-powerful in his embraces holds.

II. MAX AND DÜRER.[29]

PRINCE, soldier-lad, knight, and swindler, in the city of Augsburg meet,
In the hall the councillors brawling, and the people in the street;
While Want is abroad in the land, here crowds in the taverns riot;
This thing, what do you call it? It is the Imperial Diet.

Max stood at the window gazing—on the tumultuous scene,
When enter'd in homely doublet a man of modest mien;
"Why, Master Dürer, God bless you!" said Max with a joyous start,
"How comes my Apelles to Babel? To the Diet how cometh Art?"

"I've only one favour to beg, my lord," the modest master said,
"And may it be kindly granted,"—and he humbly bow'd his head;
"I would once more paint your portrait, and make of it, in sooth,
The double of its original, in honesty and truth."

The emperor in sadness his hand to the artist extends:
"With me 'tis the dusk of evening, and before dark night descends
You'd be glad to show the landscape in the shadows of twilight
drest,—
Well, friend, if that's your desire, I cheerfully grant your request."

Placing the palette and canvas, the painter his pencil took:
"Yet one thing I pray, my emperor, away with that austere look!"
Max's eye, fix'd on the canvas, with a sudden emotion flashes,
"As dark as the face of your canvas, my thoughts are of dust and
ashes."

The painter plies his pencil. Mouth, cheeks, nose, looks are there,
And the emperor for laughing falls backward in his chair:
"Ha, ha, there, how defiantly the faithful canvas shows,
As like, as in a looking-glass, my formidable nose."

And colour on colour brightens, as blossoms in spring-time blow,
And the life and breath of spring-time through the circle of colours
flow;
Out bloom the colours caressing the lips with a genial smile,
Enthroning with sober earnestness the sombre brow the while

"Ah, there is the man entire, the mansion true and old,
And at one of its windows, Sorrow with its chill, sad glance, behold;

Joy stands nodding and smiling at this other window of mine,
For this house nothing remains now but to hang out the crown as a
sign!

"Farewell, now, brother Albert! I well may call you brother,
A king am I, and a king you are, as good as any other;
A stick of gold my sceptre, some green land my domain,
While you, in the realm of your canvas, with a brush for a sceptre—
reign!

"The colours of the rainbow your faithful subjects be,
And truer they have been to you than ever mine to me;
And Life is the aim of my powers, and yours is still the same,
And both in toil and trouble pursue the path of Fame.

"And when we have once succeeded, and think we have finished
quite
Some task wherein we have laboured unwearied by day and night,
Comes in some dunce of a fellow, who looks with a jaundiced eye,
And says,—'It's a so-so likeness,—the throne stands a little awry.'

"God bless thee, brother Albert! Pray with my greeting call
Upon Hans Sachs at Nuremburg, the man of rhyme and awl;

When again he writes a poem, a requiem let it be;
You'll soon hear a king who is dear to you is dead,—say this from
me."

So speaks the Prince, and sadly looks the honest man in the eye,
And long with a mild expression regards him silently;
The crown'd and gilded portrait then contemplates for a while,
And smiles on it as one who would rather weep than smile!

III. DEPARTURE.

MAX would ride forth from Augsburg. But indeed it hardly
suits
The rider who starts on a journey, to start without hat or
boots;
His the women of Augsburg had stolen, that he might be forced to
remain,
But by dancing a measure to ransom them, Max came by his own
again.

Max rode from the gates of Augsburg. But it is not pleasant to
find,
When thou ridest forth from a city, that thy heart remains behind;

So over the road of the Lechfeld he pensively took his way,
Till he reach'd what is call'd the Rennsaulé, a pillar ancient and grey.

There Max drew in his bridle, and turn'd his horse quickly round,
For one more look at the city, which to him was hallow'd ground;
"My faithful and loving Augsburg! there thou liest in the morning light,
Thou canst not divine, the joyous, my spirit's sorrowing night.

"Thou divinest not that with blessings my looks on thee I bend,
And thou canst not return the greeting which to thee I fondly send;
As buried in dreamless slumber the child is never aware
That the father bends over the cradle, and whispers his blessing there."

And then three times he cross'd himself, and utter'd reverently,
"Farewell! and may God's blessing, my Augsburg, rest on thee;
May He thy tried fidelity and thy true love repay,
May He defend thy ramparts, and be thy people's stay!

"For the last time we meet now, and so for ever farewell;
Many true friends await me, who in beautiful Tyrol dwell;

Then brighten up, my countenance, and mine eye no more be sad,
From friend to friend to be going, believe me, is not so bad.

" Thus the quiet realm of spirits may I sometimes wander through,
And with serene heart, severed my well-beloved from you,
Enter the blissful circle where Love my coming attends,
And cries, It is not so grievous to be going from friends to friends!"

The Prince.

TRANSITION.

IGH on the ridge of a mountain stands a tree of the evergreen race,
Alone it stands, and no second appears far and wide in space;
Like the stalwart form of a giant, that cedar its branches rears,
A mountain its trunk—on a mountain! its foliage a forest appears.

That giant his evergreen branches lifts proudly to the sky,
As if he dared to knock boldly at the gates of the most High:
As a veil he wears the clouds which he seizes in their flight,
And the sun on his head he places as a crown of golden light.

The rosy Dawn his servant, through a path of gold and fire,
Comes first, his form in a mantle of purple to attire;
And when with its last glad greeting the sun sinks in the west,
Comes Evening of his purple the giant to divest.

Thou standest on thy mountain—thou lofty cedar tree,
And in all the realm thou beholdest there is no peer for thee:
Thus prince in life thou risest, the crown-resplendent man,
Thus also in life thou standest—King Maximilian!

Hark! the majestic rustling through the cedar's swaying limbs,
In an earnest spirit chorus hear the everlasting hymns;
Like an anthem of the ages resounding far and wide,
While in its solemn echoes it drowns all songs beside.

My song, oh Max! be hush'd now—for me it were not meet,
To sing how thou guid'st thy people from thy imperial seat;
For who would willingly listen to the minstrel's modest strain,
When the jubilee of a nation rings out in wild refrain!

Of many deeds of the ruler must the strings be silent now,
How before thee in the council thy loyal people bow;
How proud thou art and resplendent in thy jewell'd diadem,
And how therein Humility shines the most precious gem;

How thy head was never shelter'd from the fury of the storm,
Yet no leaf torn from the garland that crown'd thy lofty form;
For often the task is graver the wreaths we have won to defend,
Than the wreaths of early victories with later bays to blend.

Thou did'st not for thy diadem at the Vatican pay court,
Should the cedar to the sun-flower appeal for its support?
On thine own head—looking to Heaven—it was placed with thine own hands,
And Heaven vouchsafed the blessing,—and firm and fast it stands!

But look to thine own tiara, Rome's bishop! and hold it fast,
For the breeze that now makes it tremble will soon become a blast;
In the dust that proud tiara is doom'd to be torn and tost,
And the Holiness soon will follow, whenever the Hat is lost!

No heretic for thee, Max! the man of Saxony
Was a hero in monk's vesture, was a knight of truth to thee,
Who boldly from Rome's service the Christian army freed;
Death is the only Pope for all, infallible indeed!

The Frenchman's haughty lily thy royal mastery knew,
The Moslem crescent glittered as a buckle in thy shoe;
And as the desert lion in the cedar's shadow dark,
So at thy feet lay crouching the lion of Saint Mark.

Again, the prince's temples Peace crowns with silver band,
And the diamond sword of Justice gleams in a powerful hand;

To Art again thou raisest in splendour the half-fallen shrine,
And around thy brow the laurels with the olive branches twine.

But not to me, the minstrel, do these high themes belong;
Hark! the tones of another lyre, that sounds a mightier song!
This lofty song thou singest in proud immortal rhyme,
Upon thy giant harp-strings, thou giant mother Time!

Where the strings of this lyre concentre, in a crown the diamonds flame,
A thousand monarchs' coffins gave the wood to form its frame;
Thereon for its golden chords thou hast sceptre on sceptre spann'd,
And a purple mantle flutters as the lyre's silken band.

Thus many a song immortal from Time's old harpstrings floats,
The thunder peal of the avalanche the lightest of its notes;
Clio sits at her foot-stool, and chronicles what she sings,
And one of her matchless songs, Max, with thy own achievements rings

To thee, oh, kingly cedar, I approach with homage mute,
And with reverential greeting at thy trunk I lay my lute;
Like a swan that has sung its death-song—there in silence let it lie,
Thy green and rustling branches embraced and shelter'd by!

But if thy towering summit is stricken by the thunder
And by the forkéd lightning thy trunk is cleft asunder,
Then a groan of lamentation shall thrill through every string,
And the last tones of the lyre shall thy solemn requiem sing.

Return Home.

I. DEATH IN VIEW

HIGH over the vale of Innsbruck, hid in a rocky nook,
Alone sat Max the emperor, with meditative look;
In the green garb of a hunter, the cross-bow in his hand,
In his cap the beard of the chamois, and around it a green band.

Hark, thou old and gallant archer! Hear'st thou not, after thy wont,
The shouts of thy following comrades, the joyous cries of the hunt?
Up! up! or wilt thou not notice how there the chamois springs,
Where under his hoof of iron his path on the precipice rings?

The hoary hunter sits there, so motionless and staid,
His curling grey locks gently on his hand uplifted laid;
His eye now fix'd and tranquil its gaze on the city bent,
Now sweeping over Tyrol, far and wide its glances sent.

The chamois now come near him, and around him crop their food,
And lie like barn-yard cattle about in the green wood;
With their lustrous eyes they look on him, so trusting and so
bold—
We know thou wilt not harm us—thou art so sick and old!

Max plucks the beard of the chamois from his hat, and the silken
band,
And drops the goodly cross-bow from his enfeebled hand:
"Farewell, ye cheerful trappings—away on the breezes sail;
Farewell, my faithful cross-bow, rest in the crypt of the vale!

"And the vigorous sport of the hunter that I follow'd with such
zest,
Even thou—even thou no longer rejoicest my wither'd breast;
For alas! alas! I feel it—I myself am hunted game,
At which Death, the grim sharp-shooter, takes his unerring aim."

When again the emperor home to the imperial palace came,
Upon the couch he threw himself, his limbs were worn and lame:
"Give me, my worthy butler, a goblet full of wine,
Forthwith—I want no better than grows upon the Rhine."

With mouth distorted bitterly Max of the goblet sips:
"Away with this acid liquor—for it sorely bites my lips;

It seems a growth of the Brocken, and not of the genial Rhine;
Fill me a second goblet with the best of all your wine."

Max sips the second goblet, and his eye with anger flashes,
To the ground in a thousand fragments the crystal cup he dashes:
"Does not Death work quick enough for you? Would you have him finish quicker,
That you seek my blood to poison with this infernal liquor?"

Soon the third goblet sparkles with pure and luscious wine,
'Twould have gladden'd the heart of a tippler only to see it shine;
As it bubbles to the surface the fragrant pearls behold,
While it smiles through its shell of crystal like a fountain of liquid gold.

The emperor takes the goblet, and for the third time sips,
And a third time ill-contented removes it from his lips:
"The drink is bitter and cutting—as though it were hemlock I quaff'd,
And Satan's self were the brewer that mix'd the poisonous draught."

Shaking his head, the butler with emphasis exclaim'd:
"This wine is of a vintage that far and wide is famed;

Look at the wine a moment! What a fragrance! What a hue!
The banks of the Rhine, believe me, a better never knew."

To himself Max mutters pensively: "The man is not to blame—
The wines are good and noble—to me all wine's the same!
No draught can give me pleasure, to me no bread tastes good,
For me the only nourishment is the Saviour's body and blood!"

The emperor left the palace, absorb'd in deep reflection,
Not far off he had a mansion in the process of erection;
Though all was going well there, for himself he fain would see,
And learn in what condition the master's work might be.

Around he looks, observing,—then cries out chidingly,
"Ye men, what sort of a snail's house are ye building here for me?
How slim are the crowded pillars! how narrow the hall and saloon!
And as dark as the cells of a prison when there's neither sun nor
moon."

"Honour'd Sir, I crave your pardon," quoth the master, cap in hand,
"Where in Christendom, God help me, doth a fairer mansion stand?
The hall is light as mid-day, and the pillars like cedars tower,
The roof stands as firm as a rock, and as light as the roof of a bower."

Then quietly the emperor: "The man is right, I see,
A little house befitteth a little family:
But I cannot look with pleasure on the building of your hands,
So I'll build me a better dwelling than a dwelling on the sands."

Therewith he calls a joiner and instructs him privately,
"Come go to work, my master, and a coffin make for me:
And let the oaken coffin in an oaken chest be laid,
And bring both to my palace the moment they are made."

The coffin stands by his bed-side, when he retires to rest,
And when he goes on a journey he takes the oaken chest,
And among themselves the courtiers are curious in vain,
To know what sort of treasures might this oaken chest contain.

Max once before his coffin in the twilight sat alone,
And by the dark house mutter'd in a deep and hollow tone:
"Oh, rider, worn with travel, thy hostel beckons thee,
So rich in thrones, oh, emperor! Lo, here thy last throne see!

"In thee, thou house of death, thus in funeral darkness hurl'd,
See all the idle gew-gaws I have gather'd in the world;"
And the treasures that around him in splendid coffers rest,
He takes with bitter laughter, and hurls them in the chest.

Therein he throws his sceptre and his jewell'd diadem,
Gold chains, rich purple mantles, and many a precious gem;
When a cap and bells toss'd suddenly in the chest from behind him
rang,
And the ponderous lid of iron fell with a deafening clang.

The emperor, flush'd with anger, sprang up and turning round,
Saw Conrad Von der Rosen with his eyes upon the ground;
Yet the eyes of Max flash'd fire, and he cried, in a furious tone,
"Away, thou tedious simpleton! Away with thee—Begone!"

Oh, true and loyal Conrad, then broke thy honest heart,
How through the soul it smote thee—that deep and cruel smart!
How the breast of the grey old servant swell'd with convulsive
sighs!
Alas! what a flood of bitterness burst forth from his old eyes!

The emperor sees him weeping, and at the sight repines;
And to a swift repentance his soften'd heart inclines;
His bitter speech he deprecates and eagerly recalls,
And with tears of unfeign'd sorrow on Conrad's neck he falls.

"Forgive! I feel it doubly—soon comes eternal rest;
For all that once with pleasure and with love my soul possest,

In a sea world-wide of fragments around extended lies,
Even thy faith's firm anchor seems rotten in mine eyes.

"The tree that loves no longer the soil that gave it birth,
Nor the nurture it imbibeth from the dew and from the earth,
Nor the breezes, which at mid-day a soft refreshment give,—
Such a tree, so help me, Heaven! has but little time to live."

The moon creeps into the chamber, and sees there hand in hand,
Conrad, the true and trusted, with the aged emperor stand:
Sees there two noble foreheads, whose story their grey hair tells,
One grey from wearing the diadem, and one from the cap and bells!

II. THE DEPARTURE FROM INNSBRUCK.

A BOAT was in waiting at Innsbruck, when the early morning broke,
And the sick emperor enter'd it, enveloped in a cloak;
The oak chest, never parted with, stood darkly by his side,
Forth push'd the boat impetuous on the river's rapid tide.

On shore the murmur busily among the people ran,
Whither in such a hurry, thou sad and grey old man?
Then back the words from Max's lips responsive seem'd to fly,
" Farewell! farewell! to Austria, I now will go to die."

He leans on the oaken coffin, oppress'd with cares profound,
To heaven he looks with sadness, and with sadness looks around;
" Thou beautiful land, sincerely and faithfully loved I thee,
Would that I knew my people had found happiness through me!"

The little boat cleaves the waters, and swift before Max's eye
The valleys, plains and mountains, farms and cities, backward fly;
What side he looks spring blessings, strength, industry and life,—
What side he listens, jubilee, and song and praise are rife.

The guns crack in the forest, the scythes in the meadows swing,
Through the valleys in thunder chorus the heavy hammers ring;
And out of the throats of the chimneys the smoke rises dense and
high,
As if the black pillars supported the dome of the azure sky.

And beyond them, laden with harvests, the fields lie golden and gay,
And the cattle joyously bleating on the Alpine hill-sides stray;
And the mills clack in the valley, impell'd by the restless streams,
While over the wheels swiftly turning a shower of silver gleams.

And around, on all the highways, see the living, pressing throng!
Here safe from harm the travellers beguile the way with song;
Beneath its rich freight creaking the carrier's axle rolls,
While in clouds of dust swift riders spring nimbly to their goals.

With flapping sails move onward, or with lusty stroke of oar,
In the stream the stout boats crossing each other from shore to shore;
With wares and treasures laden, Max's sailors when they meet,
Proud of their charge, their brethren will hardly deign to greet.

See there before the farm, which in freshest pasture lies,
A peasant says a blessing o'er his child with joyous eyes;
And teaches it in trouble its heart to God to raise,
While he, with hands uplifted, for all good princes prays.

And on the banks stand cities, with ramparts white and neat,
Industry hums in the dwellings, and Thrift flaunts in the street;
Greeting him from the windows, many bright faces appear,
And the bells, from the steeples chiming, ring praises in Max's ear.

Still he leans on the oaken coffin, his head with old age bent,
With blessings he looks above him, and around him with content;
He feels the thrilling answer these mute voices have express'd,
And asks no more, if his sceptre has render'd his people bless'd.

III. THE WILL AND TESTAMENT

AT Wels, in the royal palace, knights and nobles were coming and going,
As the tide of life in its avenues was restlessly ebbing and flowing;
In armour and golden doublets, in steel and in silken vest,
All on their tiptoes creeping to the prince's chamber prest.

There the emperor lay dejected, propp'd up in his sick bed,
On his wither'd arm reposing his grey and trembling head;
His bleach'd face dimly lighted by the waning fire of his eye,
As in the pallid moonlight an altar's ruins lie.

Fix'd and speechless as the statues on the tombs of royal dead,
So stand the weeping nobles by the side of Max's bed;
Even Conrad at such mourning! The lusty Rosen here!
In merry Rosen's heart's cup there lurketh many a tear.[30]

There stands the gallant Freundsberg with the smoke of battle dun,
And there, with wrinkled forehead, stands Pfinzig, Wisdom's son;
And Charles, the imperial scion—in the freshness of his bloom,
Already fix'd and sinister, his downcast look of gloom.

There stands the Dietrichsteiner,[31] his heart with mourning tried,
Whom Maximilian loved so as he loved none beside ;
Like a twin star his spirit with Max's spirit glows,
His heart, a holy temple, only Max's image knows.

The dying emperor graspeth his friend's hand cordially :
" What pledge of truth for thy truth shall I bequeath to thee ? "
" My Lord,"—thus rings the answer—" grant only, when I die,
That at thy feet my ashes in a lone grave may lie."

Raising himself the emperor nods with a gentle smile,
And his inmost soul is quicken'd with new energy the while ;
His eyes once more inspired with the ancient lustre flame,
And his lips with their old vigour his testament proclaim :

" Peace is in all our lands—to the ord be Lthe honour and glory !
For the Lord's peace also yearneth the old man tired and hoary ;
Soon, soon, before His dwelling I shall stand with dizzy eye,
And pass through crystal portals to light and peace on high.

" Upon my coffin suffer no jewell'd crown to shine,
No sceptre and no purple and no heraldry of mine ;
Be a white cross, pure and simple, embroider'd on my pall,—
Let that adorn my coffin—the coat of arms of all !

" In a hearse to Neustadt carry my ashes without parade,
And to its worthy burghers my last adieux be said!
There sometime stood my cradle, there shall my coffin rest,—
The dead child sleeps so peacefully upon his mother's breast!

" In the Castle Chapel at Neustadt, under the altar stone,
There let my corpse be buried—dust, dust with ashes strewn!
Where over my heart in sacrifice the ministering priests may bend,
And floating over my ashes the prayers of my people ascend.

" The pressure and the tempest of fate have driven me forth,
From the orient to the sunset, and from the south to the north;
Yet my native fields with gladness I see once more to-day,
To this spot all my journeys were but a longer way!

" But thou, oh Charles, my grandson, approach thou nearer me,
And list to the words that Truth from the mouth of Death speaks
to thee;
For woe to the lips where cunning lurks in the latest breath,
And woe to the lying countenance that cozens even in death.

" Of blood, of love, already Death has torn the links away,
On thy head, my nearest kindred, my diadem I lay;

Think as thy hands the diadem from the hands of Death receive,
Thou, too, ere long that diadem in the hands of Death must leave.

" This many a one has forgotten, by mad conceits misled,
Woe to him ! like a circlet of iron it galls his head ;
The fool, indeed, thinks truly, the crown is a heavy weight
But it's a heavier burden to bear men's scorn and hate.

" On me the crown press'd lightly—on me it left no wound—
Or haply 'twas hid by the laurels, about my temples bound ;
For right and faith and courage were the legends of my life,
My sword and heart, true comrades, in the hours of darkest strife.

"Thou art call'd to other conflicts, where the sword will be left behind,
A battle of thought is coming, and the warrior will be the mind ;
In the minster of Wittenberg preaches a priest in a friar's frock,
And the prince of monks at the Vatican on his old throne feels the shock.

" A new cathedral rises superbly in the land,
Watching with weapons of light, there the holy champions stand ;
On the gates write the wise man's adage, in a scroll to be read of all,
' If the word of God it will flourish, if not, it is doom'd to fall.'

"A little flame falls on the altar, to a blaze the little flame grows,
Now a giant column of fire, with the colour of blood it glows:
Oh, fear not the flame purely kindled, that heavenward may aspire,
Oh, never was earthly mansion consumed by a heavenly fire!

"Then thought, from the flame emerging, sweeps purified to light,
And soars to the empyrean! Oh, hamper not its flight!
For thought, like the sun-seeking eagle, unchain'd, uncheck'd must be,
And then to the sun in the zenith it will mount like the eagle free!

"Then on Life's highest places wilt thou with blessing go—
Seem calm when the flames of sacrifice about thee wave and glow;
Seem calm when hearts and worlds are compass'd about with night,
And in its wild encounter Life struggles with affright.

"And now upon thy forehead, my Charles, my hands I lay,
And for God's blessing on thee I reverently pray:
On the blood that courses through thee God's benediction rest,
Thy breath, thy look, thy heart-beat, thy word, thine all be blest!

"Be bless'd through sturdy vigour—be bless'd through energy—
Which as God's arm uplifted in the tempest sweeps the sea—
Arrests the fall of the avalanche and the vaulted heaven sustains,
May it fill with true nobility the blood that swells thy veins!

"May'st thou be bless'd through clemency! Which as the flower
delights,
As the air dries the tear of sorrow, as fruit the pilgrim invites;
As dew cools the sweat of labour, as around graves the moonbeams
swarm,
Be it this that with true nobility thy soul may raise and warm!

"May'st thou be bless'd through wisdom! The all-creative power
That has built this earth—huge charnel house! and upheld it to
this hour;
That race on race it cradles through the ages' trackless flight—
May wisdom thy heart illumine, and guide thy judgment right!

"May'st thou be bless'd with Love, which, as the dove on the wing,
Like a green branch from heaven to earth has borne the spring;
Love like a chain of roses binds human hearts together,
And binds like a chain of diamonds the upper world to the nether.

"Love as the blue of the atmosphere doth the ball of earth enrobe,
Love beats as the pulse of life beats, in the centre of the globe—
Love that on the world in ruins shall stand with God alone,
May Love with its fire inflame it and make thy heart its own!

"May thy race be crown'd with honours to the latest generations,
Alike in light and number to the heavenly constellations;
A spring with blossoms laden, rich with hope for the seasons to come,
An autumn of golden fruitage, that bringeth the harvest home.

"My benediction on you—to all I bid adieu.
Call the priest for the last sacrament, my pious friends and true;
That the crown might press less heavily he once anointed my brow—
For the light garland of cypress let it be anointed now!"

Knight Venturesome.

(DER THEUERDANK.[32])

HE early dawn serenely is shining on all the land,
Max sits in his velvet arm-chair, with a volume in his hand:
In the book of daring adventure and of chivalry he reads,
Of his own wild life the swan-song—the mirror of his deeds.

He reads in his achievements! the messenger of Death
Even now floats over Austria, to receive his parting breath.
He reads in his achievements! Here, princes, turn your eye,
Learn what no monk can teach you, oh, learn like him to die!

He reads how Rashness sent him, the young presumptuous squire,
In sport to the edge of the precipice, through the flood and through the fire;

And how Mischance the assassin hurl'd the rocks athwart his path,
Set the lion to destroy him, and stirr'd the tempest's wrath.

He reads it and looks upwards, and to God he gives the praise,
Who triumphantly through dangers had borne him all his days;
Through trouble and through pressure—and a victorious strife,
With nature and the elements—the crowded fray of life!

He further reads how Envy, sharp, sinister and grey,
From his head the crown and laurel wreath had gladly torn away,
Sent hosts by land and sea his dominions to invade,
Mix'd for him draughts of poison, and sharpen'd Murder's blade.

He read and search'd his bosom, and praised the manly power
Which so nobly had sustain'd him in Passion's stormiest hour;
Which in the strife of hearts made his own great heart victorious,
And in the strife of weapons, made his own good sword so glorious.

And still he reads. All blooming the distant times draw near,
And crowds of youthful images before him re-appear;
His ancient comrades rising from their graves are marshall'd there,
And the red of morning greets him—freedom and mountain air!

With a green wreath of myrtle, in bridal robe of white,
The princess Honour rises to the youthful emperor's sight;
Then shineth Max's forehead bright as the morning's ray,
He gently sobbeth " Mary!"—" Mary" dies on the air away.

Athwart his placid countenance a smile serenely plays,
Down his cheek from moisten'd eyelids a lucid tear-drop strays;
His hoary head recumbent sinks slowly on his breast,
And on his knees descending both hand and volume rest.

With the book of his life before him he sits in his velvet chair,
All motionless and silent his people find him there;
About his lips irradiate the last smile mildly glimmers,
And on the verge of his eyelids the latest tear-drop shimmers.

The old man's lifeless body his people kneel around,
In solemn silence bending their faces to the ground;
Behold the heartfelt homage to a prince's ashes paid!
What need of martial pageant or funereal parade?

It was night, dark night for Austria, the day that Max departed,
The eyes of all were dimm'd with tears, and all were broken-hearted;
Yet no owl shrieks, and no comet sweeps the skies with lurid flashes,
No storm spreads desolation, and no town is laid in ashes.

No! shining beam the heavens, fresh the vernal breezes blow,
Full of crops the fields are standing, full of vines the hill-sides glow;
Green lie the woods and meadows, and crystal the clear streams run,
The larks to the day-break carol, and the eagle mounts to the sun!

Hard by the castle of Neustadt, in a joiner's house a song
In doleful notes resounding, may be heard the whole day long;
The ancient master sings it from the earliest dawn of day,—
Blanch'd are the lips of the singer, and his scanty locks are grey.

For more than half a century the world has roll'd along,
Since the morning for the first time was a listener to this song;
Two lives since then to their limits have been wafted on Time's wing,
The one was the life of a burgher, the other the life of a king.

The path of the king is varied and rich in storied deeds,
Where gloom succeeds to sunshine, and calm to storm succeeds;
The burgher's days glide calmly, remote from care and strife,
Who knows his this day's business, as well knows all his life.

Enters the joiner's shop a man whose mien his errand tells:
"Up, master, for the corpse of Max arrives to-day from Wels;
Hark! the bells announce its coming, and priestly dirges greet,
You must build forthwith a catafalque for a royal funeral meet."

The joiner piles the scantling a catafalque to rear,
From the same scantling fashion'd there stands a cradle near;
Around fly the chips and splinters, saw creaks, and hammer rings,
Meanwhile his old-time ditty the grey-hair'd master sings:

"Whither, thou sad companion, and, cripples, whither ye?
Whither, ye riders? Whither, thou sailor of the sea?
Oh, sailing, limping, riding, all are bound to Kingdom Come,
While I am making coffins for you and me at home!"

NOTES AND ILLUSTRATIONS.

THE RULER'S CRADLE.

NOTE 1, p. 4.

EONORA, wife of the Emperor Frederick III., was the daughter of King Edward of Portugal, and mother of the Prince Maximilian, whose story is told in these poems. The marriage of this imperial pair was not a happy one, as may be readily imagined, if the husband were such as the historians describe him—mean, suspicious, indolent, dull, false, changeable and penurious. This is the contemporary account; and with the later writers, as pitcher is emptied into pitcher, the mixture loses nothing of its bitterness. Such an inventory of vices might well enough excuse the pious but somewhat unconjugal gratitude with which Leonora thanks Heaven that the boy is altogether different from his father.

AUSTRIA AND BURGUNDY.

NOTE 2, p. 12.

Frederick seems to have had an early conviction that his son Maximilian would find a desirable match in Mary of Burgundy. He broached the matter to his friend Pope Pius II., when the boy was only four years old; and in the hope of thus uniting the rich domains of Burgundy and the Netherlands to the

House of Austria, he listened complaisantly to the ambitious projects of Charles the Bold for founding the new kingdom of Burgundy. Negotiations on this subject led to the famous meeting of the two princes at Trèves, where Maximilian accompanied his father. Here Charles was thinking of his coronation, and Frederick of the marriage treaty for his son; while Louis XI. was intriguing to defeat both, with the double view of humbling a too powerful vassal, and securing the hand of Mary for the Dauphin. The emperor was willing to do all that Charles desired after the marriage; and Charles was willing to promise the hand of his daughter after the coronation. Both were ready to bargain, but neither would give credit for the price. Meanwhile the French king suggested to Frederick that Charles would not rest contented with the title of king, but was really aspiring to the imperial crown; a suggestion to some extent favoured by the more than regal splendour that Charles affected in his dress, service, and surroundings. The duke had made all his arrangements for the coronation. He had brought to Trèves a golden crown, a royal sceptre and robe, military insignia and other appropriate decorations. An imperial and a regal throne, with slightly different elevations, had been erected in the Church of the Holy Virgin; both hung with silk draperies stiff with gold, and on both sides numerous seats richly adorned for the chief nobility. All was ready for the ceremony, when Frederick astonished the world, if not the duke, by taking French leave; merely sending him word that his presence was required at Cologne, in consequence of difficulties between the Archbishop Rupert and the chapter of the cathedral, and that the subject of their late negotiations could be arranged at some future time.

These ecclesiastical troubles terminated in open hostilities. The archbishop courted the assistance of the great duke, the chapter appealed to the emperor. Charles invested Neuss with a well-appointed army of 60,000 men. Germany sent 80,000 men under the command of Albert of Saxony, to raise the siege. Desperate fights took place before the city. The Pope intervened. A truce was agreed upon. An interview followed between Frederick, who had remained at Cologne, and the Duke. Peace was restored. The adjustment of the differences between the archbishop and the chapter was referred to the Vatican. What else was stipulated no one knew; but it was generally believed that at this interview the duke formally contracted that his only daughter Mary should become the wife of the imperial prince Maximilian.

The fall of Charles at Nancy put an end to the dreams of a kingdom of Burgundy, and of an imperial crown; but during his life-time the preliminary interchange of tokens between Mary and Maximilian had opened the way for that aggrandizement of the House of Austria, the hope of which had been Frederick's inducement to attend the conference at Trèves.

For a detailed and elaborate account of the interview at Trèves, see Kirk's History of Charles the Bold, ii. pp. 189-209. See also Pontus Heuterus, *Rerum Burgundicarum*, Lib. v. Cap. 8; *Geschichte der Regierung Kaiser Maximilians des Ersten*, von D. H. Hegewisch, pp. 19-22; and *Geschichte des Kaisers Maximilian I.*, von Karl Haltaus, pp. 9-13.

NOTE 3, p. 18.

It is said that Mary at her father's suggestion replied favourably to a letter addressed to her by Prince Maximilian, and, in pledge of her faith, sent him a diamond ring. Though the duke left Trèves in a towering rage with the emperor, he was always warm in his praise of the young arch-duke, and his words had made a deep impression upon his daughter.

Pressed by her council to select from the dozen suitors for her hand, she replied coolly, "I understand that Monsieur my father, (whom may God absolve) consented and agreed to my marriage with the son of the emperor, and I have not thought of having any other than the son of the emperor." When this report was brought to Louis of Bavaria and the Bishop of Metz, whom the emperor had sent as his ambassadors to solicit the hand of "Madame Mary" for his son, they lost no time in communicating it to the Prince, who forthwith left Vienna for Frankfort, where he was received by the deputies of the states, and a crowd of knights, prelates, and princes. The Dowager Duchess of Burgundy, knowing the probable state of his purse, had been thoughtful enough to send the prince a present of 100,000 guilders, to defray his travelling expenses.

A magnificent reception awaited him at Ghent. The young and handsome prince was much admired as he rode on a brown charger, in a harness of silver embroidered with gold under a coat of red and white velvet, with a circlet of pearls and precious stones on his bare head, from which the golden locks flowed over his shoulders. He was at once conducted to the palace, where the contract was soon concluded, though it is said the lovers had no common tongue in which they could converse,—for Mary did not speak German, and Maximilian at that time was not very well up in his French.

The nuptials were celebrated two days afterwards. In his description of the marriage procession the author has kept in view the series of engravings on wood, known as the "Triumphal Procession of the Emperor Maximilian," executed probably at his suggestion by Hans Burgmaier, a pupil of Albert Dürer.

Note 4, p. 23.

A house stood in the Wallnerstrasse in Vienna, in which an old painting represented the wolf preaching to the geese.

Note 5, p. 26.

Bella gerint alii, tu felix Austria nube,
Nam quæ Mars aliis, dat tibi regna Venus.

THE EAGLE AND THE LILY.

Note 6, p. 27.

When Louis XI. was assured of the death of Charles at Nancy, he determined not only to occupy Burgundy at once as a fief of the crown, but to take possession of the other states of the duke to which France could set up no such pretension. Disappointed in his plan of uniting the Dauphin to Mary of Burgundy, a lad of eight years to a lady of twenty, he revenged himself by ravaging her territories, corrupting and betraying her ambassadors, exciting her subjects to revolt, seizing some of the fairest of her cities, negotiating treason with others, and menacing the total extinction of the Burgundian power.

After the marriage of Maximilian, there was a truce, and there was a talk of peace. Louis, however, would not abandon his spoils, and summoned the dead duke, as he never dared to summon the living, to answer before the Parliament of Paris on a charge of rebellion and felony. As the dead duke did not appear, however, he called upon the duke's daughter and her husband to answer in his behalf. As they appeared no more than the duke, he arraigned Mary of felony for advising the cities of Burgundy not to submit to France.

Naturally enough, there was no solution of this matter but an appeal to arms. Frederick invoked the aid of all Germany in behalf of his son. Maximilian took the field at the head of 20,000 men, including his German cavalry, and 300 archers furnished by Edward IV. of England. Marshalling his forces at St. Omer, he invested Terouenne, which was occupied by a French garrison. A French army under Crevecœur was despatched to raise the siege. The two armies met on the field of Guinegate, on the 7th of August 1479. Maximilian's order of battle was a square, with his German cavalry on each wing, the English archers and the arquebusiers in front, and 14,000 Flemish lancers, under Count Romont of Savoy, occupying the centre. Crevecœur and Tercy, at the head of 11,000 of the French *gendarmerie*, fell upon the German cavalry with great violence, and completely scattered them, pursuing the fugitives to the gates of Aire. Thinking the rout complete, the next thought was of booty; and the archers composing the French centre, with the valets and vivandières, abandoned themselves to the pillage of the arch-duke's camp. Meanwhile Maximilian, seeing the overthrow of his cavalry, with the *sang froid* of a veteran, threw himself into the ranks of his infantry, and falling on his knees traced the Cross on the ground, kissed it while repeating his Pater Noster, and called the whole army, nobles and soldiers, to join him in this act of adoration. The arch-duke then led an attack on the archers, while Count Romont advanced the lancers, among whom were some two hundred Flemish gentlemen, and Count Engelbert of Nassau brought into the fight some squadrons yet unbroken of the German cavalry. A frightful massacre ensued. Crevecœur returned from the pursuit in time to share in the disaster. His cavalry were worn with fatigue and encumbered with plunder, and could only save themselves as they best might, or perish under the swords of the victorious foe. Maximilian exposed himself with more recklessness than became a commander, was three times in imminent peril of his life, and once narrowly escaped being taken prisoner.

The French abandoned their booty, and their camp, with its artillery, provisions and baggage. The chief Flemish gentlemen, whose valour had contributed largely to the glory of the day, were knighted upon the field.

See the extract from the Memoirs of Jean Sire de Dadyzéle, in the Appendix to Delapierre's translation of the *Wonderlyke Oorloghen van den doorluchtigen hochgeboren Prince Kaiser Maximiliaen:* and Pontus Heuterus, *Rerum Austriacarum*, lib. i. cap. 9.

NOTE 7, p. 29.

The extreme penuriousness of Frederick was well understood. Comminen describes him as " le plus parfaitement *chiche* homme, que prince ny aultre qui ait esté de nostre temps."

NOTE 8, p. 40.

Philip I, styled the Handsome, was born at Bruges 23rd June, 1478, and married Joanna, heiress to the crowns of Castile and Arragon. From this marriage sprang two princes, afterwards emperors, under the titles of Charles V. and Ferdinand I., the ancestors of the Spanish and German lines of the Hapsburgs. Philip died at Burgos, 25th September, 1506, of a fever brought on by drinking freely of cold water, when heated in a game of tennis.

Gustave Bergenroth alleges that it was the general contemporary opinion that he was poisoned.

Prescott considers it fortunate for Ferdinand the Catholic, father-in-law of Philip, that the circumstances of his death were too notorious and too well-attested to admit of any such suspicion.

Writing some three centuries nearer the event, Pontus Heuterus is more guarded in his expressions than the decipherer or the historian. " Divers were the opinions of men," he says, " in regard to his death, and with the vulgar it was attributed to various causes, of which, as we can affirm nothing positively, we think it best to be silent; lest by imprudently giving currency to rash opinions we should, to credulous men and women prone to adopt sinister interpretations, afford ground for injuring somebody's reputation. For there are some persons who dared to say that poison was given to him by men of no small consideration at that time."—*Rerum Austriacarum*, lib. vi. cap. 10.

LOVE'S PARTING.

NOTE 9, p. 41.

In March, 1481, Mary of Burgundy, in a hunting party in the environs of Bruges, was thrown from her horse, and died of the injuries received in the fall three weeks afterwards. The Flemish chronicle, already cited, gives a simple and touching picture of the last scene. See chapter 74 of the *Wonderlyke Oorloghen*.

NOTE 10, p. 43.

Philip before-mentioned, and Margaret of Austria. The latter, born in 1480, was married, when not two years old, to Charles the dauphin of France, and by him repudiated when, as Charles VIII., he wished to annex to his crown the domain of Anne princess of Brittany, and took the princess as his wife. Margaret afterwards married Don John, heir to the Spanish throne, who died in a few months, leaving her an august widow of twenty years. Philibert II., duke of Savoy, was her next short-lived husband; and again a widow, she was appointed, on the death of her brother Philip I., governess of the Netherlands. In her administration she displayed eminent proofs of energy, prudence, and capacity, till her death in 1530. See the *Correspondance de l'Empereur Maximilian et de Marguerite d'Autriche, sa fille, gouvernante des Pays Bas*, edited from the original MSS., by M. Le Glay, and published by the Société de l'Histoire de France, in 1839.

NOTE 11, p. 44.

John Trittheim, an eminent historian and theologian, distinguished for his learning and piety, born in 1462, was elected Abbot of Spannheim at the age of twenty years. Noblemen, prelates, men of letters, and princes from all parts of Italy, France, and Germany, sought his society and conversation.

But the very powers which induced this homage exposed him to the charge of necromancy and sorcery; and Augustin Lorcheimer relates, in his *Treatise on Magic*, that Trittheim sought permission of the arch-duke Maximilian to bring his wife before him, whose death had driven him almost to despair. Maximilian consented, and retired to a private chamber with one of the principal gentlemen of his court and the magician, who forbade them on pain of death to utter a single word. Mary of Burgundy appeared to them in all her beauty, and arrayed in her usual fashion. Maximilian satisfied himself that there was no illusion, and being no longer able to doubt that his wife was before him, he was seized with a sudden fright, and by his gestures commanded the magician to cause the phantom to disappear. He obeyed, and was forbidden to attempt anything of the kind in future.

"Thus it is," says the Abbé d'Artigny, "that they dared to calumniate the Abbé Trittheim, one of the most learned and laborious writers of his age, whose whole life was animated by piety and religion. His singular treatise on the art of writing in cipher made him pass for a magician in the eyes of the vulgar, and there were not wanting well-educated but too credulous people, who judged the same of him, especially in the 16th century, when they thought they saw sorcerers all about them. The explanation that has been given of the *Stenographie* of Trittheim proves that he was no more of a magician than all the great men whose apology has been given by Naudé."—*Nouveaux Mémoires d'Histoire, de Critique, &c.* iv. 22.

MAX AND FLANDERS.

NOTE 12, p. 48.

William, Count of Arenberg, or of Mark, with the *sobriquet* of the Boar of Ardennes.

NOTE 13, p. 48.

In the belfry of Ghent, a high tower near the cathedral, erected in 1183, hang three bells, to which the inhabitants give the name of Roland, each bell weighing 11,000 pounds, one bearing this inscription :—

Roland, Roland, als ich kleppe, dann ist Brand,
Als ich luye, dann ist Oorloghe in Vlaenderland.

NOTE 14, p. 49.

France, by secret emissaries, first instigated and encouraged the rebellious movements in Flanders, which she afterwards openly sustained.

NOTE 15, p. 49.

The states of the Netherlands, except those of Flanders, recognized Maximilian as the guardian of his children. The Ghenters, however, having possession of their persons, affianced Margaret to the Dauphin and sent her to France; and keeping Philip in close custody administered the government in his name. On this, Olivier de la Marche observes—"My lord, the archduke resembles St. Eustace, from whom a wolf stole his son and a lion his daughter."

NOTE 16, p. 51.

The story of this walk in the wood is told by Dr. Joseph Grünbeck in his *Life of Maximilian*, where he devotes a chapter to the "ingenious capture of the fortified city of Tarmundt."

Flanders being in open insurrection, Maximilian was obliged to take up arms, and his first expedition was against Dendermonde. At Mechlin he constructed three waggons, which he filled with the most daring youths in his service. In one waggon they were dressed like nuns, with painted faces, and the Lady Abbess in their midst, caressing a little dog. In another, they played the part of monks; and in the third there was a group in citizens' clothes, with short swords under them. In this disguise they proceeded towards Dendermonde; and when they reached the gate and the Abbess was parleying with the sentinels for admission, the others leaped from the waggons, and, repulsing the small guard, which they took by surprise, effected an entrance. On an agreed signal Maximilian, who was posted in the vicinity with a small troop of horse, rode up full speed to the gate, and after a sharp skirmish, in which several citizens were slain, penetrated to the market-place, and took possession of the town. The war thus opened resulted in the submission of the rebels, and Bruges and Ghent consented to recognize Maximilian as the governor of Flanders and guardian of his son, on condition that the latter should not leave the Netherlands. His entry into Ghent was triumphal. Philip with many of the nobility came out to meet him. "The son did not know the father," says Olivier de la Marche, "but when he approached, the father kissed his son, and the son burst into tears."

MAXIMILIAN, ROMAN KING.

NOTE 17, p. 56.

There had been for some time among the prince-electors a desire to raise the Arch-duke Maximilian to the dignity of King of the Romans. The emperor opposed it, but nobody knew why. Perhaps the ostensible reason was the real one, when he said, "I know Max better than you do, and I tell you he is not a man of business." But the emperor changed his mind of a sudden, and one day, early in 1486, the electors at his suggestion convened at Frankfort to go through the ceremony of an election.

There was a great afflux to Frankfort on that day of nobles and clergy; dukes, counts, princes, and barons; margraves and landgraves, abbots, bishops, and archbishops; learned doctors as ambassadors from absentee princes, and counsellors or nuncios from Nuremberg and Cologne, and a dozen other cities. And the names of all of them—Hohensteins and Hohenzollerns, Schencks and Broschencks, Starenburgs and Stubenburgs, Obersteins and Katzenelnbogens, Sonnenbergs and Schwarzenbergs—fill with their euphonious vocables at least half-a-dozen folio pages of FREHER. And all these gentlemen, with their sometimes conflicting claims of precedence, they managed to arrange in a procession for marching to the church of St. Bartholomew. But it was an act of grace worth mentioning, that the Prince of Brandenburg, on account of his age and infirmity, was permitted to enter the church in advance, for fear of the pressure of the crowd. Leaving the rest to get in as they may, we will merely note that there was such a display of magnificent dresses, collars, and bracelets on the occasion, that the chronicler could not enumerate them in a day's time.

On the south side of the altar, where the epistle was usually read, seats had been erected for the emperor, the prince-electors, and the arch-duke; and the highest of them was occupied by Frederick, in his crown and imperial robes. On the right hand were the Archbishop of Mayence, Philip of Bavaria, Count Palatine of the Rhine, and Maximilian, Arch-duke of Austria and Duke of Burgundy. On the left were the Archbishop of Cologne, Ernest, Duke of Saxony, and Albert of Brandenburg. One of the prince-electors was conspicuous by his absence; for Frederick, fearing his dissent, had not invited the attendance of the King of Bohemia.

Solemn mass was said at the high altar. The *Sanctus* was chaunted; at its commencement, the crown was removed from the head of the emperor, and replaced at its close; while the sword, apple, and sceptre were removed and placed in the hands of the three secular electors.

These ceremonies over, the prince-electors approached the altar to be sworn, and immediately went into conclave to elect a King of the Romans. The election was made with one voice. Counts and princes were called in, promiscuously, to witness it. The Archbishop of Cologne, the Count Palatine, and the Duke Ernest of Saxony were sent to inform Maximilian of their choice, and introduce him into the conclave. Hence he was conducted after a short delay, and mounted upon the altar, while the organs and a thousand voices burst forth with *Te Deum laudamus*. The chaunt finished, the secretary of the Archbishop of Mayence, by special commission from the electors, made publication of their choice, and commanded due obedience to Maximilian, as King of the Romans.

After a few days' sojourn in Frankfort, the prince-electors with the emperor and young king, attended by a distinguished company of counts, barons, and other nobles, departed for Aix, where they were to assist in the coronation. They stopped *en route* at Bingen, and afterwards at Rense, where they placed Maximilian, after the old custom, in the king's seat; a high stone, situated without the walls of the town, on the banks of the Rhine. There was the usual programme for a royal party,—processions, presents, feasts, and masses,—through Andernach, Cologne, and Duren, till they made their solemn entry into Aix. Five days were required to make the arrangements, and the 9th of March was announced as Coronation Day.

The ceremonies commenced by roasting an ox before the King's hotel. Within the ox was a pig, and within the pig a goose, and within the goose a hen. From the ox a slice was cut for the king, and then the people fell upon it with swords, knives, and sticks, each striving to consume more than his neighbour. Before the palace a bronze fountain was erected—with a black eagle bearing the arms of the Roman king, a golden lion with the arms of Brabant on one side, and a black lion with the arms of Flandria on the other; all spouting streams of Rhenish wine. Here was the popular rendezvous of poor men and rich.

The coronation took place after the old fashion. There was a great procession of nobles, secular and clerical, and much show of scarlet and red velvet with gold embroidery, and flashing jewels in caps and mantles; in which the prince-electors were almost as conspicuous as the emperor or the king. As they approached the entrance of the cathedral, they were met by the spiritual prince-electors, with their mitres and crosiers, in full pontificals. A priest attended them with crosses, a censer, and a copy of the Evangelists. Prelates, bishops, and abbots swelled the circle. Offices, collects, chaunts and benedictions followed Maximilian to a throne before the altar of the Virgin Mary. Mass was said; and the king, having laid aside his outer garment, prostrated himself in the form of a cross before the altar. Two clerks commenced singing the Litany, when the Archbishop of Cologne rose with his crosier in hand, and said: *That thou mayst be pleased to elect thy servant Maximilian a king.* The clerks responded: *We beseech thee, hear us.* The archbishop continued: *That thou mayst be pleased to bless, raise, and consecrate him.* Response as before; and so on to the completion of the Litany, when the king rose, and the archbishop standing before the altar questioned him on six points: if he would be true to the Holy Catholic faith, the defence of the Holy Church and its ministers, the just government and effective defence of the kingdom, the preservation of the laws of the kingdom and the empire, and the honest administration of their effects; even justice to the poor and rich, and the protection of the widows and orphans, and his due subjection to the holy father in Christ, the Roman Pontiff and the Holy Roman Church. To all of which inquiries he gave the anticipated affirmative response; and being then led to the altar, placed on it two fingers of his right hand, and swore: "In so far as I shall be sustained by divine assistance, and be strengthened by the prayers of faithful Christians, I will faithfully fulfil all the premises, and may God help me, and all his saints!" Being again placed before the altar, the archbishop presented him to the assembled princes of Germany, the clergy and the people, and asked with due circumlocution if they would accept him as their King; to which they responded—*Be it so!*

They then led the king to the altar, where he prostrated himself at full length on the ground, and remained so while the archbishop pronounced an elaborate benediction over him. This finished, they raised him upon his knees and stripped his shoulders and breast, and the joints of his arms; and as he knelt with his hands clasped in the attitude of prayer, the archbishop poured the holy oil upon his head, breast, between the shoulders and the arm-joints, the archbishop saying *With the holy oil I anoint thee as king, in the name of the Father, and the Son, and the Holy Ghost.* The palms of his hands were then anointed; and after appropriate chaunts and choruses, the king was attended to the sacristy, where the elders of the chapter rubbed off the anointed places with the finest wool. This done, the lords of the chapter clad him in sandals and a white robe; and returning before the altar, he again prostrated himself in the form of a cross. Again collects, benedictions, and chaunts, and a beautiful prologue by the archbishop, when the prelates put a cap on the king's head, and presented a naked sword with an appropriate speech; which finished, they replaced the sword in its sheath and belted it on the king. With another speech the Archbishop of Cologne then delivered to him the ring, the bracelets, and a mantle. Again, with a speech, the Archbishop of Cologne delivered the sceptre and the regal apple. This concluded, the three spiritual prince-electors the Archbishops of Cologne, Mèchlin, and Trèves, all three together placed the crown of Charlemagne on his head, each repeating the formula, *Receive the crown*, &c. The king was then conducted to the altar, on which he laid his two hands, and made profession to the people of his intent to reign righteously, and to render due honour to the Pope of Rome and the Roman Church. This profession made, the king was conducted to his throne or the very royal stone seat of Charlemagne, before the altar of the Apostles Simon and Jude, where, holding the sword of Charlemagne in his hand, he made some two hundred knights. Sceptre in hand, the king approached the offertory, and threw in a handful of gold coin, followed by the Archbishops of Trèves and Mechlin, and by the secular prince-electors. Thus the mass was said, down to the Pax, when the Archbishop of Cologne turned towards the people and bestowed his benediction on the king. The king was then admitted as a prebendary in the Church, and gave the admission-wine according to custom, appointed vicars to represent him, and thus ended the Coronation.

Then came the grand procession to the town hall where dinner was prepared. The nobles took the lead, counts and barons in great numbers followed; trumpeters and heralds; prelates, bishops and princes; the electors of the empire—first the Archbishop of Trèves, second Ernest Duke of Saxony, with a naked sword before the king; on his right Philip Count Palatine with the golden apple; on his left, bearing the sceptre, the representative of the Margrave of Brandenburg who had died. The king with sword on thigh, and wearing the royal crown, with the Archbishop of Cologne on his right, and the Archbishop of Mechlin on his left, in the vestures and ornaments appropriate to their electoral rank; and the Emperor in his crown and cap, attended by his herald. And as they went to the town hall, money was scattered among the people in the king's name—Rhenish florins to wit, and silver pieces to the value of three hundred florins—no very large sum even for those days; but the king was poor, and the emperor parsimonious. But the people, we are told, ran after the money rather than the king.

At the town hall was the great banquet given by the king to the princes. When the procession arrived, Ernest of Saxony, with a silver measure and a silver staff in his hand, mounted his horse, and drove him breast-high into a huge pile of grain that was collected in the market-place. The silver measure he filled with grain and handed it to one of his followers. His office thus fulfilled, the crowd rushed in, and the grain was soon scattered broad-cast through the market-place.

In the hall there was a table raised above the rest, and covered with a cloth richly inlaid with the arms of Burgundy, for his imperial majesty and the king. When they were ready for dinner, the bishop-elect, Augustensis of Hohenzone, in the place of the deceased Prince of Brandenburg, preceded by Ernest of Saxony with a black rod, brought napkins and water in silver ewers. The three archbishops asked a blessing; and taking the seal from the imperial chancery, they placed it with a rod before the king. Duke Ernest, with his black rod, preceded the Count Palatine, Prince Elector and Dapifer of the Roman Empire, to the king's kitchen with four silver dishes in his hands. The Count Palatine returned on horseback to the town hall, dismounted, ascended the steps, and placed the dishes on the table of the king. And after the prince-electors had discharged their several offices, each of them sat down apart at the table prepared for him, indicated by his own coat of arms.

How the barons, prelates and princes, and the rest should be arranged, with due regard to their several claims for precedence, was a matter to which the chief marshal no doubt was obliged to address his whole mind. The fifth place had been assigned to the consuls of the city of Frankfort, and the sixth to the consuls of Nuremberg. The Nurembergers applied to the marshal to know why the Frankforters had been assigned the higher place. The marshal replied that he found it so written down in his register. But not content with this they appealed to the king, who responded—"Since in Frankfort we were elected king, for this occasion the Frankforters must stay where they are—we will think of precedence and places another time."

But as the exhausted historian of the day's events observes—Who can tell all? Enough, that there were courses numberless, and the dishes were always full—there were roasted hares, lambs and peacocks, and all manner of birds, beasts and fishes, and the finest and most precious wines. And while the princes were despatching all these dainties within, the poor without were not forgotten; but received through the windows bread and flesh, including lambs and hares roasted whole; and we are told there was great clamour in the market-place. In the hall there was great silence and decorum, for Maximilian was no friend to revelry. And when the banquet at an early hour was finished, napkins and water in silver ewers were again brought to the royal and imperial table, and the three archbishops returned thanks—and there was an end to the Coronation Day.

De Coronatione Maximiliani Regis Romanorum, iii. FREHER, *Rerum Germanicarum Scriptores*, pp. 22-41.

THRONE AND TRIPOD.

NOTE 18, p. 59.

During the regency of Maximilian, Flanders remained in a state of chronic discontent, sometimes breaking out into open revolt and insurrection. It was, therefore, in opposition to the advice of his wisest counsellors that the king accepted a friendly invitation of the authorities of Bruges to pay them the visit at Candlemas in 1488, which resulted in the scenes described in the text.

NOTE 19, p. 74.

The citizens had affixed the following chronogram on the door of the Kranenburg: "reX. non. est. hIC. eCCe. LoCUs. Vbi. PosVerVnt. IpsVM."

ST. MARTIN'S WALL.

NOTE 20, p. 77.

St. Martin's Wall is a stupendous precipice of the Solstein mountain, descending to the very bank of the Inn. In pursuing a chamois on the rocks above, the imperial hunter lost his footing, and rolled headlong to the verge of the precipice, where he clung, head downwards, to a ledge seemingly inaccessible. So desperate was his position that the abbot of Wilton offered up prayers at the foot of the rock for a person on the point of death. As he lay there without hope, commending his soul to heaven, he was roused by a loud *halloo* from a hunter named Zips, a poacher, who had fled to the mountains to avoid prosecution for his offences. By the daring efforts of this man he was rescued from a position so perilous that the common people to this day attribute his deliverance to supernatural interposition. A crucifix eighteen feet high, placed in a recess cut in the rock, marks the scene of this occurrence. The emperor's pension list, still extant, shows that sixteen florins annually were paid to one Zips of Zirl, the picturesque village at the base of the mountain; and tradition there says that Maximilian rewarded his preserver with the title of Count Hollauer von Hohenfelsen.

MAX BEFORE VIENNA.

NOTE 21, p. 82.

Matthias Corvin, King of Hungary, the most illustrious monarch of his age, had been for thirty years the plague of the emperor, and had overrun Austria and taken Vienna in 1485. Frederick was unwilling to pay the 700,000 florins he demanded for the evacuation of his territory; and the more so as the astrologers had predicted the king's death in 1490. In that year it occurred. The widow of Matthias seems to have contemplated the settlement of the difficulty by a marriage with Maximilian; but when he addressed her reverently as his "good mother," she ceased to be sanguine on this point. Maximilian raised an army of several thousand men, and entered Vienna amid the acclamations of its citizens. The citadel, occupied by an Hungarian garrison, resisted successfully two storming parties, in one of which the king who led it was wounded. On the tenth day the garrison surrendered, and its fall was followed by the early surrender of other strongholds and the expulsion of the Hungarians from Austria.

GERMAN USAGE.

NOTE 22, p. 90.

Frederick III. passed his last days at Linz, engaged in the study of astronomy and alchemy; and died there in August 1493 Soon afterwards Maximilian, as emperor, convened the Diet at Worms, where among other things he promulgated the famous ordinance for abolishing private wars, styled the "Treuga Dei." It was at this time that the French knight De Barre came to Worms, and by the mouth of a herald challenged the Germans to a single combat. He was famed for his prowess in such encounters, and no one dared to accept his challenge. Maximilian therefore resolved to enter the lists himself, and fought the Frenchman with the lance first, and afterwards with the sword. De Barre with a thrust fissured the emperor's armour, and wounded him slightly—whereupon Maximilian set upon him with so much vigour that he called for quarter, and promised to render himself prisoner at the court of his conqueror. It was whispered at Worms that De Barre had been sent by the French Court.

KNIGHTS AND FREEMEN.

NOTE 23, p. 95.

The incidents of this imperial campaign in Switzerland are related by Billibald Pirkheimer, "the German Zenophon," in his *Historia Belli Helvetici*, iii. FREHER, pp. 67-90.

Their victories over Charles the Bold had given the Swiss great military reputation, and ambassadors from all the powers were negotiating for their friendship Maximilian tried every means to secure them, but they would acknowledge no allegiance to the empire, and the one thing needful the emperor was not able to produce. *Peint d'argent, point de Suisse;* and while other powers only promised, France paid, and with France the Swiss continued to cast their fortunes. War was the consequence. This was the last attempt to dissolve the Confederation and attach it to the wheel of the empire. The Swiss came out of the struggle with greater glory than ever.

NOTE 24, p. 99.

A Dieu mon ame,
Ma vie au roy,
Mon cœur aux dames,
L'honneur pour moi.

NOTE 25, p. 103.

In the battle of Frastenz. like Winkelried at Sempach, Henry Wohlleb of Uri, a brave and veteran soldier, pushing his long halberd transversely under the spears of half a dozen of the enemy, lifted them with great force into the air, and thus held a passage for his comrades till he fell covered with wounds. At the same battle of Sempach, Nicholas Gutt, mayor of Zofinger, who carried the banner, tore it in pieces, to prevent it from falling into the enemy's hands; and was found after the battle under heaps of the dead with the staff of the banner between his teeth. Since then the mayors of Zofinger have been sworn to guard their town-banner as well as did Nicholas Gutt. See J. von Muller's *History of the Swiss Confederacy*, Book II. and Pirkheimer *ut supra*.

THE FIGHT AT THE GRAVE.

NOTE 26, p. 115.

This episode in Maximilian's history is known as the War of the Bavarian Succession. By conquest and inheritance, Bavaria had fallen under the jurisdiction of two dukes—George the Rich, of the Landshut line, and his cousin Albert, of the line of Munich. They made a covenant that if either should die without male issue, the survivor should inherit his estates; but when George found that Albert was likely to survive him, he thought this taking an unfair advantage, and on his death-bed shocked his ghostly advisers by the gross abuse of his cousin. In these last days, he left by will all his vast possessions to his daughter Elizabeth, wife of the Palsgrave Robert, son of the Elector Palatine; and, having formed secret alliances with the kings of France and Bohemia, swore the most daring of his vassals to fealty to his son-in-law.

But Albert looked on the matter in a different light; and, having a friend at court in Maximilian, whose sister Cunigunde he had married, he called on the emperor to aid him in enforcing the covenant. Maximilian accepted the opportunity of administering on this large estate, and not the less readily, perhaps, because he had some claims of his own against it. Albert at the same time made friends with the Suabian League, with the margrave Frederick of

Brandenburg, the landgrave William of Hesse, and the city of Nuremberg. The duke Ulric of Wurtemburg he secured by the promise of his daughter in marriage, with a portion of 200,000 guilders, to be paid no doubt from the estate in controversy.

Maximilian now held a Suabian Diet at Ulm, where he enfeoffed the Duke Albert with the lands of his deceased cousin. In spite of this decision, Robert entered into the possession of Landshut, including Burghausen and the treasures of gold, silver, and precious stones which had been amassed by three acquisitive generations, and which were said to exceed by far those of any other German prince.

So another diet was called--this time at Augsburg. The parties appeared by attorney, and there was an elaborate discussion of the feudal right of female inheritance. It was obvious enough,—the suggestion of the Canon of Bamberg on Robert's behalf,—that through this right the emperor himself had acquired some of his fairest possessions. Maximilian took all this in good part, and did his best to effect a compromise. Failing in this, he called in the president and assessors of the Chamber of Justice, to assist the princes and electors in reaching a proper decision. The result was another judgment in Albert's favour.

But Robert made as light of the Diet of Augsburg as of the Diet of Ulm. He thought possession nine points of the law. With Burghausen and its treasures in hand he could defy the empire, and by protracted hostilities worry out the somewhat impecunious Albert. By a huge bribe, he induced Pinzenauer to betray the strong castle of Kuffstein. He scattered money with both hands. Opening the war in Lower Bavaria, he carried everything before him at the start. The troops of Albert deserted for the want of pay, but new allies came to his aid. Many bold barons found they had cause of grievance against the elector Palatine, and on one side or the other nearly all Germany took part in the quarrel. Less than a year, however, sufficed to disperse all the treasures of Burghausen—the coinage of the colossal silver statues of the twelve apostles inclusive. Fevered and exhausted by the excitements of the conflict Robert died suddenly. His wife, who was of the same fiery temper, and who had appeared in the camp in boots and spurs, armed with a battle-axe, followed him before many days.

They left two children, heirs presumptive to the pretensions of Robert. In their behalf, Philip, the elector Palatine, took the field with some thousand Bohemians, fell upon the Brandenburg provinces, burned down some towns, and shut himself up in his castle at Heidelberg, which was strongly fortified.

The war now raged with barbarous fury in the Palatinate. Towns and villages, to the number of one hundred and fifty, were sacked and burned, and all the country about Heidelberg was laid waste. Maximilian came down the Danube with a numerous force, and met the Bohemians, in the pay of the Count Palatine, at Mengesbach near Ratisbon. On his approach the enemy burned their tents, and posted themselves on an eminence behind a barricade of waggons, in front of which they had erected a fence with their shields, spiked in the ground and joined together by chains.

Prince Casimir was sent, with 400 cavalry and eight Nuremburg field pieces, to attack them on their right flank and dislodge them; but he met with so warm a reception that he was glad to leave his eight pieces on the field, and fly to the nearest wood. Maximilian then headed in person a charge at full speed on the centre, and was engaged in the thickest of the fray,—was turned in his saddle, and was on the point of losing his life or his liberty. From this imminent peril he was rescued by Eric of Brunswick, who was himself wounded in the encounter, and carried out of the battle to Ratisbon. The Bohemians formed into small squares of sixteen men each, and fought with desperate courage, but were finally routed with terrible slaughter. Six hundred were taken prisoners; and, as an offset to the capture of their cannon, the Nuremberg boys bore off seven standards in triumph. Maximilian rewarded his preserver by adding a golden star in a peacock's tail to his coat of arms, and giving him for life the income of the county of Gortz.

Maximilian now besieged the castle of Kuffstein, situated on a high rock overlooking the Inn, on the borders of Tyrol and Bavaria, in command of the same Pinzenauer who had betrayed it. He opened on it with seven batteries in vain, for the walls were fourteen feet in thickness. They yielded, however, to the knocks of Purlepaus and Wakeup, and Pinzenauer sought permission to withdraw. This was refused, on the ground that he had wantonly compelled the unnecessary destruction of the fine castle. To this may be referred the cruel judgment executed on a portion of the prisoners taken after a siege of fourteen days, the incidents of which are substantially described in the verse.

The fall of Kuffstein precipitated the close of the war. Philip consented to submit the matter in dispute to the next diet, which was held at Cologne. The ban of the empire was lifted from his head, and a universal amnesty declared. Provision was made for the sons of Robert, from the *débris* of the Burghausen treasures and certain territorial rights in what was called the Young Palatinate. Albert's allies, the landgraves and margraves, the dukes and reverend clergy, and the city of Nuremberg, took a town or a castle, or both, here and there. The emperor did not omit to indemnify himself for the time, trouble, and money expended about the business. He took numerous lordships and castles, including Kuffstein, and adjusted in his own way all the accounts, whether of money or territory, outstanding between Bavaria and the House of Austria. What remained, satisfied the Duke Albert of Munich.

NOTE 27, p. 124.

Maximilian prided himself on his artillery, in which he introduced numerous improvements. He loved his cannon as other men love their horses. Besides his two favourites, Purlepaus and Wakeup, we read of the Nightingale, the Tickler, the Singers, the Grumbler, and others with names equally significant. In three beautiful volumes on parchment, in manuscript richly painted and gilded, preserved in the Ambras Collection in Vienna, Maximilian has collected drawings and descriptions of the imperial artillery and ordnance. Almost every cannon has its name, and German rhymes playing upon it, written on the drawing.

THE LAST VICTORY.

NOTE 28, p. 130.

In 1513 Henry VIII. of England took up arms for the Pope against France, and, collecting a large army, crossed the Straits to Calais, and laid siege to Terouenne. Maximilian, on the spur of the moment, raised several squadrons of horse and foot, and by forced marches hurried from Germany through Belgium to the English camp. On the way he was joined by re-inforcements levied by his daughter Margaret, regent of the Netherlands.

The English army invested the town in three divisions. On the east, Henry was pressing the siege in person, Talbot on the south, and the Duke of Somerset on the west and north.

Henry met Maximilian at St. Omer, saluted him as "father," and accepted his services as a volunteer, with the pay of an hundred crowns per diem. The next day they made together a *reconnoissance* of the fortifications, and of the ground in the neighbourhood. While thus engaged, news was brought to them that the King of France would within two days send on all his cavalry from Amiens, with provisions for the relief of the besieged. It was determined to cross the Lis, and meet them on the way.

Talbot remained before Terouenne. The rest of the forces passed the river on extemporized bridges, and were formed in two divisions, the horse under the command of Maximilian, Henry and Somerset taking the lead of the infantry. The emperor, in a few words of encouragement, reminded his troops that the ground was the scene of one of his old victories; and that though his beard and hair had whitened since then, his heart was as red as ever, and promised that they would find him when they followed in the thick of the fight. The Germans, who first knew of his presence in the camp when he lifted his helmet to speak, received him with repeated shouts of enthusiasm. Meanwhile the French cavalry to the number of 8000 under the Duke of Pienne were approaching, with the pack-horses and waggon-trains loaded with provision, in their midst. They were veteran troops, victors in many battles. Maximilian advanced his horse, Henry following at a rapid march with the foot-soldiers. When they were near Guinegate, the signal of attack was given by sound of trumpet; and dashing his spurs into his horse, the emperor with his usual reckless valour rushed upon the enemy, and unhorsed a French knight. The French ranks could not withstand the impetuosity of the onset, and were thrown into utter disorder, in spite of the gallant and persistent efforts of their leader to rally them. They broke and fled, leaving several of their distinguished captains prisoners, who were ransomed upon the spot. The flight became a rout. The Duke of Pienne escaped with small loss to Blangy, where he received the fugitives. Most of their standards were captured. They lost all their provisions, artillery, and baggage. Pontus Heuterus, whose account we have followed, mentions that in his youth he had heard old men say that it was called at the time the Battle of the Spurs.

MAX IN AUGSBURG.

Note 29, p. 145.

When Maximilian held his last diet at Augsburg, Albert Dürer was present, and painted his portrait. At the same time he made a half-length sketch in black chalk, preserved in the collection of the Archduke Albert, at Vienna, and inscribed in Dürer's hand :—"Here is the Kaiser of whom I, Albert Dürer in Augsburg, high in the palace in his little chamber, made the counterfeit, 1518, on the Monday after John the Baptist."

Dürer was held in the highest esteem by Maximilian, who knighted him, and conferred on him the title of painter to the Imperial court. In honour of his benefactor and friend, the artist, besides the admirable portrait engraved and published shortly after the emperor's death, designed "The Triumphal Car of Kaiser Maximilian I.," representing in a series of engravings the gorgeous chariot of the Kaiser, drawn by twelve horses, led by nymphs representing the Virtues, while victory crowns him with the laurel-wreath. The "Triumphal Arch of Kaiser Max" is a tribute on a larger scale, proving perhaps no less the encouragement that the emperor was disposed to bestow upon art, than the zeal with which the artist devoted himself to commemorate the reign and the race of the emperor. This work was engraved on ninety-two blocks, an immense labour, that must have occupied many artists for several years. The second impression of the work as completed was edited by Bartsch at Vienna, in 1779.

THE RETURN HOME.

Note 30, p. 165.

Conrad von der Rosen, the court fool and faithful life-long friend of the emperor, survived him. See Karl Flogel's *Geschichte der Hofnarren*, pp. 190-203. (1789.)

NOTE 31, p. 166.

Sigismund von Dietrichstein was one of the dearest friends of the knightly emperor, and is buried at his feet, under the altar of the Gothic Chapel of St. George, in the old Ducal Castle at Neustadt.

KNIGHT VENTURESOME.

NOTE 32, p. 172.

Der Theuerdank, which may be translated " one who meditates adventures," is an allegorical epic of knight errantry, whose hero, Maximilian himself, is involved in a series of adventures by three inimical allegorical personages, to wit: Fürwittig (Indiscretion, Youthful Rashness); Onfallo (Mischance, Hostility of the Elements); and Neydelhart (Envy, Malevolence, Misanthropy). He triumphs over them all, however, in the long run, and wins for his bride the beautiful princess Ehrenreich (Rich in Honour) Mary of Burgundy.

This poem is said to have been written by Melchior Pfinzing, one of his secretaries, from biographical memoranda written or dictated by the emperor himself. The Nuremberg edition of 1517 is a typographical master-piece. It is decorated with numerous engravings from designs of Hans Burgmaier and Hans Schaufflein. The impression so closely resembles a MS. that many printers have thought the effect could have been produced only by the xylographic process. Similar perfection was attained by Schœnsperger, printer to the emperor, in the Book of Hours, of which ten copies were printed on vellum, one of which, with beautiful designs by Albert Dürer, exists in an unfinished state in the library at Munich.

www.ingramcontent.com/pod-product-compliance
Lightning Source LLC
Chambersburg PA
CBHW020616030726
47497CB00007B/2272

9783337064730